THE CHEEKY MINX

MERRY FARMER

THE CHEEKY MINX

Cover design by Erin Dameron-Hill (the miracle-worker)

ASIN: B07PQ23H1C

Paperback ISBN: 9781090687500

Click here for a complete list of other works by Merry Farmer.

If you'd like to be the first to learn about when the next books in the series come out and more, please sign up for my newsletter here: http://eepurl.com/RQ-KX

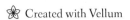 Created with Vellum

For Cissie...a free woman!

CHAPTER 1

LONDON – AUTUMN, 1815

*W*hen the scandal surrounding Miss Dobson's Finishing School broke like a wave crashing upon the shore of London's high society, Miss Josephine Hodges was elated. Finally, the haughty mothers and indifferent fathers who had shunted their daughters off to such a horrible school—which was really more of a reformatory for young ladies ages eighteen to twenty-two who had embroiled themselves in some kind of scandal—when they should have been having their first or even second season, would see the light.

Miss Dobson was little more than a conniving shyster who took advantage of the young ladies entrusted to her in the best of times and outright abused them in the worst. Jo and her closest friend, Lady Caroline Pepys, had witnessed their other bosom friend, Lady Rebecca Burgess, in the aftermath of a humiliating punishment only a fortnight before, and it had nearly broken Jo's heart. At least Rebecca had been rescued by the ruggedly handsome Bow Street Runner, Mr. Nigel Kent—who, as it turned out, was actually Baron Wharton and a peer.

"We should all be so lucky as to accidentally marry peers," Caro said to Jo as they sat on cold, hard benches in one of the school's classrooms, embroidering cases for pillows. Caro stabbed her work with a vicious scowl that Jo could only assume meant she was picturing Miss Dobson's face.

"But you're the daughter of an earl," Jo pointed out. "Surely you will marry a peer."

Caro laughed and stabbed her embroidery again. "To hear my mother talk, I'll end up a disreputable spinster."

Jo very much doubted that. Caro was too pretty and far too clever to end up a spinster. That was a fate she was certain belonged to her alone of all her friends. Not that she begrudged them.

"I'm happy for Rebecca," Jo said with a sigh, picking out a row of stitches she'd done wrong. Embroidery was such a silly, useless occupation. If she had to be at a school at her ripe age of nineteen, she would rather have been learning History or studying literature, not doing the same boring thing she would be doing if she were still at home. Not that she wanted to be at home anymore, not with the way her mother continually looked at her in disgust after "the incident".

2

"I'm happy for Rebecca too," Caro admitted, stabbing her work again. "And I dare say a bit jealous."

Jo hummed. "Yes, Mr. Kent—I mean, Lord Wharton —is a handsome man. And the letters Rebecca has managed to sneak to us via Flora have been so delicious. Can you believe Mr. Kent let her measure his manhood that way?"

Caro snorted, then glanced around to make sure none of the other young ladies working with them were listening. "I'm more surprised by the measurements. Good heavens, to have a man like that." She paused in her work to fan herself.

On the benches across from them, Miss Felicity Murdoch and Lady Eliza Towers met Caro's eyes across their messy work, then exchanged a grin and a giggle.

"What?" Lady Ophelia Binghamton whispered, looking as though she'd missed a passing parade. "What are we talking about?"

"Ladies," Miss Dobson snapped from the front of the room, where she sat behind a desk, poring over ledgers. "Silence!"

Jo and Caro exchanged a look before Caro sent an apologetic look to their friends across the way. Felicity and Eliza returned the look with one of bored camaraderie, while Ophelia continued to look lost.

When silence reigned once more and they had all continued with their work, Caro whispered, "What I wouldn't give for a man with an enormous cock."

That sent Jo, Felicity, Eliza, and even Ophelia into a

flurry of poorly-suppressed laughter and snorting. The laughter was contagious, and within moments, even the pupils who weren't sitting close enough to have heard Caro's bold comment started giggling.

"Stop that noise this instant," Miss Dobson shouted, smacking one of her ledgers on her desk, "or I'll lock you all in your rooms without supper and rap your knuckles until they bleed!"

Jo did her best to resume a sober air, as did most of the others. Felicity and Eliza had a hard time keeping their mirth under wraps, but they managed to swallow and go on with their work.

In fact, Miss Dobson's threats no longer had teeth. Jo peeked around the room at her fellow inmates. Within the last fortnight, enrollment at the school had been cut in half. The eighteen young ladies who remained were all Miss Dobson had to rely on. As soon as word of her treatment of Rebecca became public, a steady stream of parents arrived at the school's door, demanding to take their daughters home.

Well, in truth, the line was made up of servants belonging to the fortunate young women's parents. Few parents came to fetch their so-called wayward daughters themselves. That only served as proof for Jo's theory that Miss Dobson's school was a prison for those unfortunate enough to be caught in scandal's web rather than a place loving and caring parents sent their daughters to gain the skills they would need to conquer society. And those young women carted off by housekeepers and lady's maids were the lucky ones. The young ladies remaining at the school had been abandoned by parents who either didn't care about the scandal or who thought Miss Dobson was in the right to use corporal punishment on one of her charges.

Jo's mother had sent a letter mildly admonishing Miss Dobson but confirming her insistence that Jo stay where she was to have her morals reformed. Caro's parents had sent nothing at all. But as miserable as those circumstances were, they still had each other, they still had secret letters from a newlywed Rebecca, and they still had the secret passageway that connected their plain bedroom on the second floor of the school with the house owned by the East India Company next door.

"I cannot wait for tonight," Jo whispered when it looked as though Miss Dobson was absorbed in her calculations once more. "The diamond thief will return to enjoy Mr. Khan's party, I just know it."

Caro hummed in agreement. "I cannot wait to get my first look at his son, Saif Khan."

The two of them exchanged grins. It was almost a month ago that the Chandramukhi Diamond had gone missing from the house owned by the East India Company. The list of suspects had been long to begin with. Rebecca's Nigel had been called in to investigate the theft, and, of course, Rebecca, Jo, and Caro had quickly become involved. Through the secret passageway, they'd managed to overhear vital conversations between the thief and his accomplices and to witness more than a few startlingly carnal acts involving the thief.

To be honest, Jo and Caro had availed themselves of the secret passages more than a few times in the last fortnight to spy on all manner of carnal acts that had nothing to do with the diamond. Jo's cheeks flared hot just thinking about the education she was getting late at night, when boredom set in. Mr. Khan, who ran the house on behalf of the East India Company, hosted frequent bacchanals, and even when there wasn't a party, he procured intimate entertainment for Company employees. Jo had witnessed sexual congress in a long list of fascinating positions through the voyeuristic peepholes that were part of the secret passageways. What she'd seen aroused and enflamed her, but it also sparked unexpected outrage within her. She'd been committed to the walls of Miss Dobson's school for far less than she now knew was possible between a man and a woman.

"If only there were a way we could mingle freely with Mr. Khan's guests without being mistaken for strumpets," Caro said with a sigh, nudging Jo out of her uncomfortable thoughts. "I'm certain that if we could simply converse with the men who were present at Mr. Khan's entertainments the night the diamond was stolen, we could lure the thief into confessing his crimes."

"We wouldn't have to do all that," Jo whispered back. "All we have to do is corner Lord Lichfield and coax him into confessing."

Caro arched a brow at Jo. "You're still convinced Lord Lichfield is the thief?"

"Rebecca is convinced," Jo said. "Because Mr. Kent is convinced. And Mr. Kent is a Bow Street Runner. He would know."

Caro shook her head. "Mr. Kent is Baron Wharton now. He gave up his position with the Runners when he married Rebecca last week so that he could take up his baronial duties."

"But he still knows quite a bit about the investigation," Jo argued.

"What he knows is weeks old," Caro said. "New information may have come to light."

Jo frowned. "You don't think Lord Lichfield is the thief?"

"No," Caro said. "I still think it's—"

"Good morning, ladies."

Their discussion—indeed, everything in the classroom—came to a screeching halt as the tall, lean, and not entirely disagreeable form of Mr. Wallace Newman appeared in the doorway.

"I'm not interrupting, am I?" Mr. Newman went on, striding into the room. He glanced from side to side at the young ladies, his eyes sharp. "How is the work coming along?"

Jo straightened, eyeing the man warily. Mr. Newman was a mill owner from the North who had come to London for business purposes. He was young for what he'd been able to accomplish, perhaps in his mid-thirties, and he wasn't unpleasant to look at. His blond hair was fashionably cut and his jaw was strong, if a little beefier than Jo preferred. Half the young ladies in the room sat straighter, making eyes at him and thrusting their chests forward. Mr. Newman feasted openly on the sights that were presented to him, and Jo could have sworn that the front of his breeches protruded more than it should. She would rather have died than flirt with Mr. Newman. Not only had she seen him in attendance at several of Mr. Khan's illicit parties, he was Caro's prime suspect in the theft of the Chandramukhi Diamond.

"Mr. Newman." Miss Dobson leapt up from her desk, rushing around to greet him in the center of the room. She patted her hair and pushed up her bosom the same as half of her pupils, even though she was a good twenty years older than the man. "How delightful to see you."

Jo could barely watch the exchange. She felt down-right ill at the way Miss Dobson flirted.

Apparently, she wasn't the only one. Mr. Newman's broad smile turned sour, and he took a step back to put some distance between himself and Miss Dobson. "I came to check on the work I commissioned," he said.

Miss Dobson swayed toward him as though he'd said he was there to ask for her hand in marriage. "They're hard at work now, see?" She gestured toward one bench of embroidering pupils.

Jo sat up straighter, her eyebrows lifting to her hair-line, then glanced down at the pillowcase she was working on. Was it all just a commission for Mr. Newman?

"Very nice," Mr. Newman said. He strode to the bench where Felicity, Eliza, and Ophelia sat and plucked the embroidery hoop right out of Ophelia's hands. Ophelia yelped. Mr. Newman studied her work with a hum, then glanced down at the expanse of Ophelia's ample bosom. "Very nice indeed," he said, like a snake about to devour a mouse.

Ophelia yelped a second time and crossed her arms to cover her chest.

"Never mind that," Miss Dobson said, grabbing his arm and spinning him back toward her. "If you've come to discuss business, perhaps we could retire to a more private room?" She batted her eyelashes at him.

Jo's stomach threatened to heave. There was no doubt in her mind what Miss Dobson truly wanted to do with Mr. Newman.

"The wheels of business are forever turning," Mr. Newman said, holding Miss Dobson at arm's length. "There is no time for dalliance," he added through a clenched jaw.

"Oh, but we have so much *business* to discuss," Miss Dobson insisted, lowering her voice and adding a salacious laugh. "So much business."

She managed to wheedle her way close enough to rub a hand against Mr. Newman's arm. She stood at an unfortunately perfect angle for Jo to see her eyes drop to the bulge in his breeches. She licked her lips.

Jo had to turn away. "This is insufferable," she whispered to Caro. "I would rather have my knuckles rapped with a switch than witness this torture."

Caro hummed in agreement, but before she could say anything, Flora, the school's head maid, stepped into the doorway and cleared her throat.

"What do you want?" Miss Dobson snapped at her.

"If you please, miss," Flora began with a deep curtsy. "Mrs. Hodges is here. She has requested that Miss Hodges join her for tea this afternoon."

Jo's eyes popped wide. She hadn't heard from her mother in more than a week. She certainly hadn't had warning that she was invited to tea of any sort. It was highly unusual for her mother—and the rest of her family —to acknowledge her at all. So much so that she sat straighter and asked Flora, "Are you certain?"

"Yes, miss," Flora told her with another curtsy. There was a light of sympathy in Flora's eyes that reminded Jo she was on her side.

Miss Dobson hissed out a breath. "This is highly inconvenient. Mr. Newman needs his embroidery by the end of the week or—" She stopped, flushing, then turned to Mr. Newman. "Really, we should discuss this elsewhere."

"No need for discussion, madam," Mr. Newman said. But he leaned closer to Miss Dobson and whispered something that brought a pink flush to the woman's cheeks and a smile to her lips.

Jo's stomach turned again, and she stood. If her

mother wanted her, at least she could use her surprise appearance as an excuse to flee the horrible scene. She sent a final look to Caro—who nodded encouragingly—then set her embroidery aside and hurried to Flora in the doorway.

"This is highly irregular," she told Flora as the two of them crossed through the hall to the front of the school. "She didn't send any notice."

"No, miss," Flora agreed. "Not a thing."

Jo would have asked more questions, but when she reached the front of the school, her mother was standing there, looking impatient.

"Ah, Josephine," she said without a hint of affection. "There you are. Come along."

Jo's heart shivered with disappointment. "Would you like me to change out of my school frock and into something more appropriate for tea?" she asked, fetching her bonnet from the long line of pegs beside the door.

Her mother looked her over, making Jo feel three inches tall. "No," she said with a sigh. "Not even the finest silks could make you any better than you are. Besides, you won't need to win anyone over where we're going. The deal has already been done."

Jo swallowed anxiously and followed her mother out of the school. Her family's carriage waited in the street, her father's driver standing ready. He jumped to hold the door as Jo and her mother descended the school's front stairs.

"What deal?" Jo asked once she and her mother were comfortably situated inside the carriage.

Her mother waited until they had lurched into motion. Even then, she straightened her skirts, tugged on her gloves, and adjusted her bonnet, doing everything possible to make herself comfortable before so much as acknowledging Jo was in the carriage with her.

At last, she said, "You're to be married."

Jo's eyes went wide and her mouth dropped open. "I am?"

"I was as shocked as you are," her mother said without directly answering her. "I'd given up hope after that appalling incident. And with the footman. Oh, Josephine," she sighed with utter disappointment, shaking her head.

Jo lowered her head sheepishly. Part of her wanted to ask how Rob was doing. Part of her wanted to forget the whole silly, embarrassing incident. It hadn't been what her mother thought it was. At least, not entirely. Curiosity had gotten the better of her, and in spite of his inferior position, Rob was a tease. It was merely horribly bad luck that her sister, Wilma, had entered the room just as Jo had closed her hand around Rob's engorged shaft. It didn't matter how much she swore that she had only wanted to know what it felt like and that nothing further had transpired.

"You will do your duty as a wife," her mother went on, thankfully unable to see Jo's thoughts. "That is all that is required of you. You will not ask questions about your husband's extramarital activities. That's what chased the last one away," her mother added in a wry aside.

"His last wife?" Jo asked, dread pooling in her stomach.

"Broken engagement," her mother said, again an indirect answer that meant she could convey information without fully acknowledging Jo's presence. "He's desperate for heirs, but now that his nature has been made public, few respectable young ladies are willing to affiance themselves to him, in spite of the title."

"Title?" Jo sat straighter. Perhaps, like Rebecca, she would be fortunate enough to accidentally marry a peer.

"Yes," her mother said, meeting Jo's eyes at last. "You are engaged to Lord Felix Harlow, Earl of Lichfield."

CHAPTER 2

"*I*'m engaged to Lord Lichfield?" Jo squeaked before she could stop herself.

Immediately, the image of him as she'd seen him three weeks ago, devilishly spanking the bare bottom of a woman at one of Mr. Khan's revels, popped to her mind. She tried reminding herself that the woman hadn't looked as though she minded being spanked at all, but that brought up a wealth of overheated emotions that were decidedly inconvenient while she was trapped alone in a carriage with her mother.

"Do not look so squeamish, child," her mother snapped, shaking her head, her lip curled in a sneer. "The man has a reputation, it is true, but considering your own reputation, I should think you would thrill at this chance."

As much as Jo told herself her mother's words

shouldn't sting, they did. "I don't have a reputation, Mama. I have never misbehaved in public."

Her mother snorted and glanced out the window. "In public," she repeated scoffingly.

A wall went down between them. The conversation was over, and Jo knew there wasn't a thing she could do to salvage her worth in her mother's eyes. One minor indiscretion, one moment of indulgence—a moment that her mother hadn't even witnessed—and in her mother's eyes, she was no better than the jades lurking around the theater. It was all Wilma's fault at that. Her sister had exaggerated the whole thing horrifically, and now here Jo was, engaged to a criminal.

She caught her breath as the carriage jerked to a stop in front of a stately, Georgian townhouse in Mayfair. She was engaged to the diamond thief. Which, of course, meant that she couldn't possibly have a marriage based on love, like she'd so hoped she would. But there were bene-fits to the mad match. She was now in a better position than anyone to needle a confession out of him and to bring him to justice. Perhaps fate had done her a favor after all.

But when she stumbled out of the carriage—without any help from her mother or the coachman, who fawned all over her and ignored Jo—they were met at the front door not by Lord Lichfield, but by a dour-faced butler.

"Good morning, madam," the butler said with a deep bow. "Lady Lichfield is waiting for you."

Jo swallowed her nerves and vowed to face whatever

was waiting for her with dignity and grace. Even though she was wearing a drab school uniform that barely had any shape itself, let alone enough to emphasize her natural shape, she walked with her back straight and her chin held high through the hall and into the parlor where the butler led them.

Her spirits sank in an instant at the sight of the woman waiting for them.

"Lady Lichfield," her mother said, sweeping into the room with all the confidence that her father's vast fortune and social connections gave her. "How lovely to see you."

"And you, my dear." Lady Lichfield stood to greet Jo's mother, pretending to embrace her and kiss her on each cheek, although Jo doubted the two women actually touched each other. "I've had Cook prepare your favorite lemon tarts."

"You are too kind," her mother said with an airy laugh. She followed Lady Lichfield to one of the two settees in the room, and both ladies sat.

Lady Lichfield was clearly cut from the same cloth as Jo's mother. She was short but managed to carry herself in a way that made her appear taller. Her day dress was of the highest fashion with accent jewelry that was worth a small fortune. That alone made Jo narrow her eyes slightly to study the woman. Perhaps Lord Lichfield stole the diamond to please his mother. Lady Lichfield kept her expression as bland as possible, which might have explained why she had fewer lines and wrinkles on her face than most women her age, as if she had made a study of not taxing the muscles in her face.

"So," Lady Lichfield said, glancing to Jo for the first time and studying her with cold eyes. "Is this her?"

"Yes," Jo's mother said. "As you can see, she is comely. She is neither clever nor inquisitive, so she will not be of trouble to you."

"I can see." Lady Lichfield tipped her head back, studying Jo down her nose. "You are correct. She does not have that spark of insouciance that I so dislike in young ladies these days."

"She will be biddable as long as you maintain a firm hand," her mother went on.

"She does not speak out of turn?" Lady Lichfield asked.

"No. If she does, an immediate and sharp correction will set her straight."

Jo swallowed, dreading what her mother meant by a "sharp correction".

Lady Lichfield's gaze swept over Jo's body. "Are her hips sufficiently wide for bearing children?"

"They are," Jo's mother confirmed. "I brought five children into this world without a problem, and between them, her two older sisters already have four."

"And she will not fuss when bedded, no matter how peculiar my son's tastes?"

Jo's cheeks burned with anger and embarrassment. Her mother and Lady Lichfield were discussing her as though she were a broodmare. Worse still, it was clear that, in fact, that was all she was required to be.

Her mother laughed. "I doubt Lord Lichfield will have a problem in that area. For in spite of my best efforts, my daughter is wanton in the extreme."

"Not too much, I hope," Lady Lichfield said, turning to Jo's mother in horror. "Her fidelity must remain unquestionable."

"I can assure you that the good work Miss Dobson is doing at her school has curbed her loose inclinations," her mother assured Lady Lichfield. "She will readily part her legs where necessary and keep them clamped shut otherwise. And if she does not, Lord Lichfield can send her abroad as soon as an heir and a spare are born."

"Perfect," Lady Lichfield said with a slight smile. "My son will be pleased."

Jo was on the verge of tears. She couldn't have imagined a worse humiliation if she had tried. A maid brought in tea on a silver service, and Lady Lichfield served herself and Jo's mother, but neither of them offered so much as a crumb to Jo, nor did they invite her to sit down.

"She isn't flighty, is she?" Lady Lichfield asked, nibbling on a biscuit once the tea was poured. "I don't want a repeat of the Lady Malvis situation."

Even that tidbit of gossip did nothing to improve Jo's flagging spirits. Lady Malvis was the daughter of a duke who had been engaged to Lord Lichfield in the spring but who had called off the engagement under mysterious circumstances. That Lord Lichfield was willing to settle for the daughter of a merchant instead of a titled lady said more about his desperation than her value.

"She will do as she's told," Jo's mother reassured Lady Lichfield, speaking as though Jo weren't there. "No matter what shocks she receives."

Jo's heart sped up, even as it sagged. There could be no doubt that the shock in question was the fact that her fiancé was a thief. Was she expected to provide the man with an heir and a spare while he languished in prison for the crime? Was that why no woman of birth and breeding would have him.

"Good morning, mother."

Her thoughts were cut short with a jolt as Lord Lichfield himself strode into the room. Prickles raced down her back, and the image of him smacking the woman's bottom rushed back to her mind. Hard on the heels of that, Lord Lichfield walked past her and into her view. He went dutifully to kiss his mother's cheek, straightened and bowed to Jo's mother, then turned to Jo.

A ripple of heat claimed Jo as Lord Lichfield smiled. Devil though he may be, he was a handsome one. He was tall and well-built, with dark hair and eyes that sparkled with his smile. His suit was the height of fashion and his cravat was tied high on his neck, but it was at that moment that Jo realized she'd been so enamored of the way he had manhandled his companion on that fateful night that she'd forgotten his shirt had been undone and part of his chest was showing. Lord Lichfield was the finest specimen of masculinity that she'd ever seen.

"Good morning," he addressed her, his manners impeccable.

Before Jo could answer, Lady Lichfield said in an offhanded way, "Felix, this is Miss Hodges, your intended."

Lord Lichfield's welcoming smile flattened a bit, and he sent his mother a sideways glance. "I have not approved of your scheme of hiring a woman for me to marry, Mother." He turned back to Jo and added, "Begging your pardon, Miss Hodges."

Jo opened her mouth to speak, but Lady Lichfield rode over her with, "She's perfectly biddable, she comes from wealth, and she will give you the heirs you need."

A flush formed on Lord Lichfield's face. "Perhaps we could discuss such delicate matters in private, Mother."

If Jo wasn't mistaken, he was angry with his mother's plotting. Which meant he wasn't a part of it. Which also meant he might cast her off. As uncomfortable as Jo was marrying a diamond thief, she couldn't help but feel the sting to her pride.

"There is nothing to discuss," Lady Lichfield said in a businesslike tone. "The deal is done. You can have the banns read or apply for a special license to wed the girl sooner, if you're in as much of a hurry to get an heir as you say you are."

"I did not say I was in a hurry to get an heir," Lord Lichfield said to his mother through clenched teeth, looking more embarrassed by the moment. "I said that I would like a family of my own."

"Nonsense." His mother brushed away his statement with a wave of her hand, which turned into pointing at the other settee and ordering him to sit. "You have a family. Me. Now sit and pour yourself some tea."

Lord Lichfield stared hard at his mother for so long that Jo began to squirm with discomfort. At last, he blew out a breath and shook his head as though he knew he would lose any argument he started. But rather than sitting, he turned to Jo. "Would you like tea, Miss Hodges?"

It shouldn't have, it truly shouldn't have, but his simple offer shot straight to Jo's heart. Especially after she had been ignored so soundly and treated as chattel by her mother and his. "Yes, please," she said in a quiet voice.

"Do sit down." He gestured toward the settee where he'd been ordered to sit before reaching for the tea things.

Jo was so grateful for the chance to sit that she almost didn't notice the shocked and offended looks her mother and Lady Lichfield had for Lord Lichfield.

"You are not the hostess here, Felix, I am," his mother said.

"And Miss Hodges is our guest," he said, smiling at Jo when she finally did manage to sit, feeling so tense that she might burst into shards at any moment. "If you have your way, she will be a very special guest."

"Really, Felix," Lady Lichfield said with a sigh and a shake of her head. "You are in no position to lecture me on propriety and morality."

Jo nearly fumbled the teacup that Lord Lichfield

handed her. Especially as Lord Lichfield seemed cowed by his mother's statement. He sat, cheeks flushed, and sipped his tea without further comment. Jo glanced between mother and son. Could it be that Lady Lichfield knew her son was a thief? But she must. The woman's air was too superior for her not to know that her son was guilty.

"Did you hear about Lady Abernathy's little mishap last week?" Lady Lichfield asked Jo's mother.

"Yes," her mother replied, eyes going wide at the introduction of gossip. "I don't know how she can show her face in polite society after that."

"She shouldn't," Lady Lichfield said.

The two older women launched into a flurry of gossip as sharp as a knife edge. Jo was too disheartened by the whole thing to pay attention. She sipped her tea in silence, grateful that Lord Lichfield had added just the right amount of sugar.

She was surprised when, a minute or so after their mothers had lost themselves in gossip, he asked, "Are you enjoying the little season?"

Jo was glad that she'd already swallowed her tea. She would have choked at the direct address otherwise. "I haven't been a part of it," she confessed.

"Oh?" He frowned. The expression was quite attractive on him. "Whyever not?"

Jo lowered her head sheepishly, but a moment later, she snapped it up again to meet his eyes. Perhaps if she were honest with him she wouldn't have to marry a diamond thief after all.

"I am currently a pupil at Miss Dobson's Finishing School," she said.

Lord Lichfield smiled and began, "Why, that's right next—" He stopped abruptly, his face going redder. "I have attended events at the house adjoining the school."

Yes, you have, Jo thought to herself. *And enjoyed them as well.*

Aloud, she said, "We enjoy watching guests of the East India Company coming and going from the house."

No sooner were the words out of her mouth when inspiration hit her. She could interrogate Lord Lichfield about the diamond without him knowing he was being questioned.

"Have you been attending events at the East India Company's house for long?" she asked before he could say anything else that might sidetrack her.

He shrugged. "Off and on since Mr. Khan took over the running of the house. It was little more than a secondary office for high-ranking company officials before that."

A zip of excitement flashed through Jo. Was that why secret passageways had been built into the house? So that sensitive meetings could be listened in on?

"And have you befriended any of those high-ranking officials?" Jo asked, scooting a bit closer to him.

"A few," Lord Lichfield answered. He sent a cautious glance to his mother, and when he saw that she wasn't interested in their conversation, he said, "I've explored a few investments with the East India Company. Their model of investing does much to limit the exposure to risk that other investing models carry with it." He paused, a smile spreading across his face. "But I'm certain a fine lady like you has no interest in investments and business."

"But I do," Jo insisted, believing it herself for a moment. "I find it fascinating. What sort of Indian things do you invest in? Tea? Textiles? Leather goods? Diamonds?"

His expression pinched for a moment, almost as though he flinched. Had she hit a nerve with her mention of diamonds?

Before she could ask more questions, another surprising revelation was made. Though she was deliberately not paying attention to her mother and Lady Lichfield's conversation, she suddenly picked up the words, "...which is why I am staying here, at Felix's house, for the time being."

Jo put her teacup down so that she wouldn't drop it in her excitement. "Is this your house?" she asked Lord Lichfield.

"It is," he confirmed with a smile. "Why? Does it not meet with your approval?"

She had the feeling he was teasing her, but she answered with an honest, "It's lovely." Then went on to say, "And do you keep all of your belongings here?"

He laughed, probably thinking her question was odd.

Jo's mother and his paused their gossip to glare at the two of them. Jo and Lord Lichfield both sent them looks of contrition, but when they returned to their conversation, Lord Lichfield answered, "Everything I keep in London I keep here. Our family has an estate in Norfolk, but I haven't been back for years." He sent his mother a wary look as if in explanation.

Jo grinned from ear-to-ear, not because he seemed to be taking her into his confidence, but because his confession meant that the Chandramukhi Diamond had to be on the premises. Why, he could have it stuffed in the cushions of the settee without anyone knowing it. She could be seated on the diamond at that moment. She wiggled a little in her seat to see if she could feel it.

It was, perhaps, the wrong movement to make. Lord Lichfield's gaze dropped to her hips, then flickered up a bit to her breasts. All at once, Jo had the feeling he was assessing her not as a polite guest for tea, but as a man sizes up a woman who was destined to be in his bed. And heaven help her, the sensations his look raised in her were as tempting as they were wicked.

"Please excuse me," she said in a whisper, standing suddenly.

"Is something wrong?" Lord Lichfield asked, standing with her.

Jo's mother let out a groan, as though Jo had upset the entire tea set while calling Lady Lichfield a string of unsightly names.

Jo bit her lip, then whispered, "I need to retire for a

moment. I'll ask the butler."

Before her mother could lecture her on the vulgarity of asking for a chamber pot while in the middle of a formal tea, Jo turned and fled the room. The beauty of her excuse was that no one would follow her and Lord Lichfield's butler would never be so indelicate as to announce that he'd given Jo directions to where she could relieve herself.

Which meant that Jo could slip quietly down the hall and around the corner to the servant's part of the house. If Lord Lichfield did have the diamond at his house, she should be able to find it in a trice. As long as she avoided servants and other householders as she did.

Avoiding the upstairs maids as they went about their business was easier said than done, however. She made it up to the first floor and managed to peek into a few rooms before she was forced to leap headlong into what looked like an unused guest room until one of the maids passed. The moment she heard the girl's footsteps fade down the hall, Jo slipped out of the room and began checking every door on the hall.

She was certain she'd found what she was looking for when she located a stately, masculine, very much lived-in bedchamber toward the back of the house. It had to belong to Lord Lichfield.

With a squeal, she shut the door and set to work, bounding across the room and throwing the wardrobe open. She was instantly hit by the rich scent of wood and spice and something distinct from all other male scents she'd smelled before. It reminded her of Rebecca's comment about the man in a wolf mask at one of the East India Company's house parties—who turned out to be Lord Herrington—and how he had smelled so good that Rebecca didn't think he could possibly be the thief. Jo breathed in, leaning toward the neat row of Lord Lichfield's jackets, wondering if she might, perhaps, be wrong about the degree of his guilt based on the glorious scent of his clothing.

But no, she couldn't let herself be dissuaded so easily. There were too many other factors pointing to Lord Lichfield's guilt. But her resolve weakened once again when she pulled open a drawer within the wardrobe only to discover neat rows of soft, folded drawers. She squeaked and moved to shut the drawer, but halfway through the gesture, she changed her mind. Instead, she leaned over, a thrill rushing through her, and brought her nose as close to the intimate garments as she could. With a naughty giggle, she breathed in, eyes closed.

Her reverie was disturbed almost instantly by the sound of footsteps in the hall. As fast as she could, she shut the drawer and then the entire wardrobe. Frantic, she searched for a place she could hide if a maid entered the room. There was a door at the far side of the room that, judging by its position relative to the wall, must have led to a closet. Jo bolted for that, throwing the door open.

She stopped and her jaw dropped as she gazed into the small closet. Several whips and flails hung from pegs along one side of the closet. A variety of shackles—some made of metal, some of leather, and some that were little more than strips of silk—hung on the opposite wall. A collection of paddles ranging in size from a cricket bat to a large spoon lined the back of the wall and the walls on the sides. Propped against the side of the closet were a few thick, iron bars with what appeared to be shackles at either end and closer to the middle. There were several other items as well that defied all description. The scent of leather and musk washed over her, confusing her senses even more.

"What in heaven's name," she murmured, taking what looked like a curious necklace with a collar and silver chains that ended with twisting clamps. She held the collar with one hand and picked up one of the clamps with the other, trying to decide if it attached to one's sleeve or if it was meant to hold some other item of jewelry.

She nearly jumped out of her skin when, from behind her, Lord Lichfield said, "If you are looking for someone to show you how to wear that, you need only ask."

elix Harlow, Earl of Lichfield, had had a sinking sensation in the pit of his stomach from the moment he walked into his morning parlor and found his mother entertaining. She'd been wretchedly disappointed in him since Lady Malvis Cunningham called off their engagement early in the summer, and she'd threatened to find him a suitable girl herself if he didn't start showing interest in the right kind of woman. He should have known she'd go behind his back to do exactly what she'd promised.

The trouble was, very few of the right kind of girl wanted anything to do with him at the moment, because he was positively dripping with all of the wrong kind of women. Women who had discovered his unusual reputation and whispered about his unique skill-set behind their fans at Almack's and at the theater. That gossip had scared Lady Malvis away. For half a moment, Felix had held onto the hope that Miss Hodges hadn't heard the gossip, didn't know about his nocturnal activities, and that she might just be the key to him putting all that behind him and living a normal, vanilla life.

But then came her comment about leather goods. Certainly, it was couched within an innocent list of commodities he might trade in. There was a chance Miss Hodges meant nothing by it at all. But she was too eager, too curious, and the spark in her eyes was too cheeky for him to believe she was ignorant. And then she excused herself on the pretense of necessity.

Felix wasn't at all surprised to find her in his bedroom. Not only that, she was peering into the closet where he kept the accouterments of his activities. He sighed to himself, his heart sagging, as the hope he'd had for putting his seedy past behind him fled. The fact that she had selected a thick, studded collar with chains leading to nipple clamps from the contents of his closet seemed to prove what she was there for. Although she did look puzzled as she studied the piece.

"If you are looking for someone to show you how to wear that, you need only ask," he told her, slipping into character as he circled around his bed and approached her.

"Lord Lichfield," Miss Hodges gasped, scrambling to shut the closet door. She still held the collar and clamps as she said, "I didn't find anything, I swear. Nothing at all."

Felix's brow knit in confusion. She'd found everything and she was still holding the evidence. Oddities aside, he remained in character, stalking slowly toward her. "So, you've heard all about me, then?" he asked, arching one eyebrow rakishly.

Her mouth fell open and for a moment her eyes glittered with a sort of triumph. "I...I suspected," she said, barely above a whisper.

"And you simply had to come see for yourself?" He moved close enough to touch her, but instead of caressing her cheek or stealing a kiss, he backed her against the door, planting his hands on either side of her and using his considerable size advantage to form a sort of cage she wouldn't be able to escape from. That was what the women who pursued him wanted, after all—to give up all control, to feel mastered and helpless.

"I...." Miss Hodges continued to fumble. Her breath came in shallow gasps that did lovely things to her shapely breasts. In fact, he thought he detected lumps in her bodice where her nipples had hardened. He hated the idea of tightening the screws of the clamps she held over what were surely perfect buds of dusky pink, but if that's what she wanted....

She didn't say anything else. Felix wasn't sure if it was because he had overwhelmed her with his presence or if she was already playing the submissive role that she expected him to honor. In the back of his head, something didn't feel right, though. There was too much innocence in Miss Hodges's eyes. She was younger than the jades who usually sought out his services. And his mother had perceived her as someone worthy of marrying him and siring the next Earl of Lichfield. Which could just mean Miss Hodges was an exceptionally good actress. She was in his bedchamber, after all.

"So," he said, keeping his tone haughty and staring at her with a practiced look of unadulterated lust. "We are to be married."

Miss Hodges made an indistinct sound before forming the word, "Apparently." She followed that with a quick, rather mad burst of giggles, which she instantly swallowed and turned into a low moan that could have been either longing or dread.

The series of sounds and the whirlwind of emotions that passed through her eyes was so charming that Felix almost broke character to laugh. But in all likelihood, his betrothed hadn't come to his room to giggle, she'd come to sample what she would be getting.

"You've discovered my secret, then?" he asked her.

Her eyes widened. "So you admit it?" she whispered.

"Of course," he answered with a casual shrug. "If we are to be husband and wife, my secrets are your secrets, no?"

Her mouth dropped open, and Felix was struck with the desire to kiss her. Not the kind of brutal, bruising kiss women usually wanted from him, but a soft, coaxing kiss that would end with her blushing and giggling and wanting more.

"You want me to become involved in...." Her words faded and she gulped.

"That's what you want," he told her. Told, not asked. That was how the game was played, after all. "I knew right away when we spoke downstairs."

"You...you did?"

Again, the innocence in her eyes gave Felix pause. But no, he knew when a woman was swimming in lust, and Miss Hodges clearly wanted him. She was too artless to hide her ardor. Although he could argue with himself that that was another sign of her innocence. It all came back around to the same thing, though. She was somewhere she shouldn't be.

"You're a cheeky little minx, aren't you?" he purred, taking the collar and clamps from her trembling hand. "Sneaking into your master's room when you're supposed to be having tea."

"I—"

"Silence," he snapped.

Miss Hodges blinked and stood straighter, indignation in her eyes. So she didn't know how the game was played after all. He reconsidered his next move, tossing the collar and clamps aside. He'd have to ease her into everything.

"My future wife is a bad girl," he said, brushing a hand along her side, then closing it around her perfect breast. He fully intended to squeeze hard, pulling her up until she was forced to stand on her toes, but, surprisingly, he didn't. Instead, he simply caressed her breast, brushing his thumb over her nipple until it was hard beneath the thin muslin of her gown. He was rewarded with a sigh that tightened his groin and stiffened his cock.

"I don't try to be," she said in a small, soft voice, her eyes pleading.

A flash of genuine desire flared in Felix. She hadn't denied his claim or protested her innocence. Beyond that, there was a story in her eyes. His bride-to-be was more than she seemed. But, of course, any woman who would slip into a man's bedchamber and open his closets must be the kind of minx he'd accused her of being.

He forced himself to focus on what she had probably come to him for. "You know what happens to naughty girls, don't you?" he asked, leaning close and whispering against her lips as he continued to knead her breast. When she shook her head, holding her breath, he said, "They are punished."

She let out the breath she'd been holding on a shivery sigh that had his cock straining against his breeches. He didn't usually want the women who sought out his particular brand of play half as much as he wanted Miss Hodges right then. The sensation was dazzling.

"Are you ready to receive your punishment?" he asked, lips so close to hers that it was torture for him not to ravage her with a kiss.

Miss Hodges merely whimpered.

Jo could barely stand, what with the way Lord Lichfield pressed against her. The way he fondled her breast—boldly, without apology—had her insides swirling into a pool of liquid heat, focused in her sex. In the back of her head, she was still indignant that he'd silenced her so harshly a moment before. But now that he was a breath away from kissing her, she could think of little else.

And then he swayed back. For a moment, the rush of cool air between them shocked her to her senses. The feeling didn't last, though. He hooked his hand behind her waist and tugged her away from the door with him, then whirled her into his arms as he sat on the side of the bed.

She was ready to snuggle against him and rest her head on his shoulder, but he growled, "Naughty girls take their punishment and beg for more."

She half opened her mouth to ask what in heaven's name he was talking about, but before she could, he twisted her in his arms and lay her, face down, over his lap.

"Have you been naughty?" he asked her.

"No," she insisted, squirming against him. Mostly because she feared she might slip off of his legs and spill to the floor entirely.

He answered her denial by gathering a handful of her skirts and yanking them up to her waist. Jo yelped as he managed to deftly expose her legs above where her stockings were fastened and backside with the movement. He adjusted the way he held her so that her skirts were tucked completely out of the way and her bare backside was fully presented to him.

"What was that, minx?"

"I'm not naughty, I'm—oh!"

She knew it was coming but she was surprised all the same. He smacked his open palm across her bare bottom, and with far more force than she expected. The blow stung sharply, leaving her breathless.

"Why did you—"

Her question was cut off as he spanked her soundly again. The pain of the blow radiated through her backside. But along with the hurt, a deeper, delicious ache grew in her sex. He spanked her again—hard—and both the stinging and the ache blossomed.

"Good girls do not sneak into their fiancé's bedchambers," he said, raining another smack on her bum. "Good girls do not play with dirty toys." He spanked again, and Jo groaned. "Are you a good girl?" he asked.

"Well," Jo squeaked, thinking about her actions honestly. "I suppose I'm not."

He smacked her particularly sharply, but the sound she made wasn't a cry of protest. Oh no, it was far too excited for that.

"Only good girls deserve lily-white asses," Lord Lichfield told her, then spanked her hard. "Naughty girls have bright red asses." He followed the comment with another spank.

Jo gulped and attempted to glance over her shoulder. "Is mine red now?"

"Not red enough," Lord Lichfield said. He smacked her again, but when Jo got a fleeting glimpse of his expression, she could have sworn she saw a twinkle of mirth in his eyes and a tug at the corner of his mouth that must have been a grin.

By then, every new blow he landed fell on her already smarting flesh, making the pain radiate through her. "It hurts," she said, wriggling against him.

"Does it?" he asked, smacking her particularly hard.

Jo squealed and answered, "Yes," as she writhed against him. It was then that she realized what the hard length pressed against her side was. Spanking her had Lord Lichfield aroused.

When he spanked her again, she decided two could play at that game. She wriggled against him, purposefully making contact with his manhood. She might not have known much, but between what Rob had told her that fateful day before they'd been caught and what Rebecca and Caro had shared, she knew her movements would cause him pleasure, which might disarm him.

Indeed, he groaned and jerked against her, but then he spanked her harder.

"Cheeky little minx," he said in a voice tense with arousal. "You'll pay for that."

He smacked her again, but this time, rather than pulling his hand away, he stroked her smarting backside. Jo winced...until he slipped his hand between her thighs to stroke her sex. She caught her breath as a powerful wave of need pulled at her and let it out in a long, "Ohh!"

"Naughty girls get wet when they're punished," he said breathlessly. "God, you're wet."

Jo tried to make a clever reply, but it came out as a wanton moan as he slipped two fingers inside of her. The sensation was delicious, and she instantly wanted more. She would do anything for more, as wicked as that made her.

"Come for me," he demanded, adjusting his hand so that he both penetrated her and rubbed her clitoris. "I want to feel my naughty wife-to-be with her stinging, red ass come when her master tells her to."

She couldn't have stopped herself if she'd wanted to, but she didn't want to. With a shuddering cry, her sex felt as though it was twisting up into an impossibly tight coil, and then it burst apart in an orgasm so powerful that it filled her entire body. Lord Lichfield groaned and slipped his fingers deep inside of her, giving her inner muscles something to squeeze as wave after wave of ecstasy filled her.

"Good God," he gasped, his thighs tense under her as if he were as moved by her climax as she was.

As the height of her pleasure began to subside, Jo latched on to her desire to get even with him once again. The time for meekness and propriety was over. There she was, draped over the man's knees, her backside bared and smarting, her sex still twitching in post-orgasmic throbs, and he merely sat there feeling smug. She could change that.

With a quick burst of energy that he couldn't have been ready for, she slipped off of his knees, rolling to the side. Somehow, she managed to catch herself on her knees on the floor. By some miracle, she took him by surprise and he didn't react as she reached for the fall of his breeches and swiftly undid them. By the time he flinched in reaction, it was too late. She had his cock in hand and was stroking it fast and hard, the way Rob had instructed her to do.

He was already aroused and didn't stand a chance. In a handful of seconds, he gasped and made a strangled sound. His groin contracted powerfully and a fountain of pearly-white liquid erupted from his tip. Jo milked him for a few more strokes until his body went limp and he fell back. He only barely managed to catch himself on his elbows as his delightfully large member began to soften in her hand.

She let go and sat heavily on the floor, catching her breath with the sting of the movement, then finding a more comfortable way to sit. Lord Lichfield reclined where he was, making no attempt to move or to hide his penis from her. Neither of them said a word. Only after the fact did Jo consider how wickedly delicious it would have been if, instead of using her hand to pleasure him, she'd climbed into his lap and sheathed him deep within her. Not that she had the skill or coordination to carry off something that momentous. No, she'd done the best she could, and now Lord Lichfield was thoroughly disarmed.

At last, still panting, Lord Lichfield sat straighter. He glanced down at himself, his clothes in disarray and now soiled, and let out a wry laugh. "That wasn't exactly a shining example of stamina and control."

Jo opened her mouth to tell him he deserved what he got, but a knock at the door had both of them tensing like cats on a fence.

"My lord," a male voice said. "Your mother is concerned. Miss Hodges has gone missing. She would like your assistance in the search."

"I'll be right there, Paulson," Lord Lichfield called. When the butler's footsteps retreated, Lord Lichfield glanced at Jo with one eyebrow raised. "This should be interesting," he said, pushing himself to stand. "Think we can make ourselves presentable enough to return to our mothers without raising suspicion?"

"No," Jo admitted, taking the hand he offered to help her to her feet. "But as we are already engaged, I doubt they can do more than glower at us. And my mother's opinion of me couldn't sink lower than it already is."

He studied her with a frown that Jo felt to the core of her soul. The puzzlement in his glance slowly turned to sadness. "I'm sorry," he said at last.

Jo was certain he meant it. What became less certain as he showed her to his washstand and offered her his hairbrush to straighten her hair while he changed items of his clothing, was whether a man of such passion, but also such kindness, ironic as it felt for her to think it, could possibly be a diamond thief.

elix lay in bed the morning after his encounter with Miss Josephine Hodges, staring up at the ceiling, at a complete loss. On the one hand, he couldn't believe his mother had arranged a marriage for him without his knowledge. Yes, she'd mentioned something a time or two at the breakfast table in the last few weeks, but he hadn't dreamed she was serious. To suddenly spring a betrothal on him when all he thought he was doing was making a token appearance at one of her mornings at home was unconscionable.

But Miss Josephine Hodges was a force of nature that he wouldn't have expected in a million years. He hadn't thought much of her at first. She was short and dressed drably. True, her auburn hair had a certain luster to it and her green eyes had sparkled more than most mousey young ladies who did their mother's every bidding. Even after her questioning had convinced him she knew all about his reputation and wanted to take a bite out of his apple, his impression of her hadn't improved, merely shifted.

It wasn't until he saw the defiance in her eyes as he initiated the sort of play women demanded from him that the tables had begun to turn, and when she had taken hold of his cock and turned him into a helpless fountain of cum with only a few strokes....

His cock hardened anew at the memory. Of course, it shouldn't have, considering how ultimately embarrassing it was for him to lose control so fast in her hands. But the women he was used to being with simply didn't react that way. They bowed to him. They pouted and simpered. They presented their backsides, all of themselves, really, for punishment. They cried fake tears of contrition and sometimes real tears of pain at a catharsis that had nothing at all to do with him. They submitted. He didn't understand them, but that didn't stop him from giving them what they wanted and getting off in return.

Miss Josephine Hodges hadn't cried. She hadn't submitted. She came hard when he pleasured her, and then she pounced on him. That little, drab, slip of a thing had his cock out and spent before he could get his bearings. And it had been delicious.

He reached under the covers, grasping his swollen shaft and working it until he was as hard as granite. Miss Josephine Hodges. Lady Josephine Lichfield. His groin tightened at the thought. She was feisty, bold, unlike the women he'd come to be associated with. Her pink bottom was perfect and soft and round. He stroked himself harder, his breath coming in pants. Had she really snuck up to his bedchamber for an illicit rendezvous? She hadn't seemed to know what the equipment she found was for. That possibility sent him closer to the edge, and he growled as sharp tension pooled behind his balls. Was it possible that she had genuinely become lost while looking for a chamber pot? If so, she had borne his pseudo-abuse bravely and still been so wet that she'd come quickly for him. Perhaps she just wanted it, not with whips and restraints, but with passion. She'd played the aggressor, milking him like—

He came with a shuddering gasp and a burst of pleasure that reverberated through his bones. Warm stickiness spread across his belly, but it was worth it. He closed his eyes as his body relaxed, and thought of Miss Josephine Hodges with a smile. She would be his wife. He should argue with his mother out of principle and refuse the match, but the thought of having Josephine in his bed was too sweet to give up.

He said as much to his friend, Rufus Herrington, a few short hours later as the two of them rode through Fitzrovia toward Regent's Park.

"It was extraordinary," he told his friend, careful not to include details that would breach the borders of privacy, for Josephine's sake. "Unlike any situation I've ever found myself in."

Rufus chuckled. "It sounds as though you've found

43

yourself in an exceptionally agreeable situation," he said. "Every man dreams of marrying a biddable bride."

"Do they?" Felix asked, one brow raised. "I'm reasonably certain my father dreamed of marrying a wealthy bride and nothing else."

Rufus shrugged. "It's eighteen fifteen. Times are freer, and men can expect more than a distinguished pedigree and a sizable dowry from their bride. Although the dowry would help," he added with a sigh.

Felix sympathized with his friend. "Still no luck on the financial front?" he asked.

Rufus shook his head. "The crops failed again this year. My steward says the land is depleted and needs to be left fallow for a few years. But if I fail to plant for as long as he suggests, my tenants will go hungry and my coffers will dry up completely. I need to marry well."

"Any luck there?" Felix asked.

"If you consider title-hunting spinsters from newly wealthy families luck," Rufus said. "Mama wants me to pick one, no matter how unsuited we are, and get on with things."

"But," Felix prompted him.

Rufus sent him a sheepish sideways look. "But I haven't given up the dream of marrying a woman I actually want in my bed. And at my breakfast table and on my arm at the theater."

Felix hummed, considering himself luckier than he ever could have imagined. It was no wonder Rufus took advantage of every bacchanal in London and kept company with an array of courtesans. He was attempting to have his fun before the clock struck midnight and duty took over.

"Well, at the very least, I can help by purchasing your townhome," Felix said as they pulled to a stop in front of a handsome, brick townhome.

"The gesture is much appreciated," Rufus said as he dismounted. He waved for a boy to come over and take their horses around to the mews, handing him a coin as he did, before they headed into the house. "But are you certain you still need the place, considering your soon-to-be state a staid, married man?"

Felix laughed as they stepped into the townhome's small front hallway. "Of course, I still need it."

Rufus moved into the tiny front parlor, then turned to face Felix with a doubting look. "Are you certain your bride-to-be would consent to you owning a discreet address intended for illicit rendezvous?"

Felix thumped his shoulder. "I fear that if my mother remains in London, Miss Hodges and I will need this place for our own rendezvous. Besides," he sighed. "I need to move my equipment out of the Mayfair house. If Miss Hodges can find it by accident, there's no telling who else might."

"Your mother?" Rufus suggested.

Felix shrugged. "Can you imagine explaining those sorts of things to your mother?"

Rufus arched one brow. "Doesn't she already know?

Didn't Lady Malvis tell her when she broke your engagement?"

Felix made a face. "Blessedly, Malvis was not specific when she detailed the reasons she could not marry me." He paused. "But that didn't stop my mother from believing me to be a deviant." He paused again, running a hand through his hair. "There is no need to confirm that assessment."

Rufus scoffed. "You're no more of a deviant than I am, than any man is. None of us are unimpeachably perfect, and there's no harm in that."

Felix thumped Rufus's shoulder once more. Few things were more valuable than a friend who saw one's faults and forgave them. He let out a breath and glanced around the parlor.

"All right. I'll take it. When do you want to have the papers for the sale drawn up and signed?"

"As soon as possible." Rufus ran a hand through his hair. "I feel as though I've already spent the profits of the sale."

"And I feel as though I've already inhabited the place," Felix replied with a lopsided grin.

Rufus laughed. "Because you have." He arched a brow. "Am I right in thinking Lady Ulster is meeting you here again tomorrow?"

Felix's grin vanished. "She's supposed to," he admitted. "She sent me a note the day before yesterday informing me that she has been extraordinarily naughty and needs to be thoroughly punished for her transgressions."

"But?" Rufus prompted.

"But my heart isn't in it anymore," Felix confessed. "I'm going to cancel the engagement and close shop."

"Am I to assume that a certain fiancée has something to do with this change of heart?"

Felix winced, rubbing a hand over his face. If he was honest with himself, his heart hadn't been in the game for months. His reputation was as stellar as ever and he hadn't let his performance flag one bit, but he no longer got the same thrill as he once did from fulfilling the secret fantasies of the ladies of the *ton*. Josephine was merely the last straw.

He opened his mouth to explain as much, but a knock on the door startled him into silence. He and Rufus both turned as the door opened and a sly-looking Indian gentleman let himself in.

"There you are," the Indian gentleman said. "Father said I might find you out this way."

"Saif," Rufus greeted the man, striding back into the hall to take his hand after he shut the door. "You're back in London."

"And ready for adventure," Saif said.

"Welcome back," Felix said, shaking Saif's hand as he and Rufus returned to the parlor.

Saif Khan was the eldest son of Mr. Wakas Khan, the man who managed the house owned by the East India Company. Saif had come to England years ago to study in the hopes of securing a position in the administration of the East India Company. But after passing his exams, he decided he'd rather stay in the modern environs of London, making only periodic jaunts home to Bombay. Felix wasn't sure he approved of his young friend. It seemed to him that the young man's expensive education could be put to better use in his homeland. Saif rarely seemed interested in being of any use to anyone at all.

"So," he said, clasping his arms around both Felix's and Rufus's shoulders, as though they were still young bucks at university. "It's a damn shame about my father's diamond, isn't it?"

Felix's brow shot up and he exchanged a glance with Rufus. "I was given to understand that the Chandra-mukhi Diamond belonged to Emperor Akbar."

Saif made a scoffing sound. "He intended it as a gift to King George, but it was my father's responsibility until such a time as the gift could be given." He shrugged. "If the gift could be given at all. In my opinion, it should have been payment for my father's services to the empire."

Felix exchanged another look with Rufus before saying, "Do you know anything about its current whereabouts?"

Saif laughed, stepping away from them and going to inspect a clock on the parlor's mantelpiece. "Of course not," he said without looking at them. "But I wish I did." He let out a longing breath. "Father is offering a substantial reward. Even if he wasn't, the kind of blunt that diamond would bring could end all of my troubles."

The hair lifted on the back of Felix's neck at the comment. "You realize that both Rufus and I are considered suspects in the diamond's disappearance," he said.

"Truly?" Saif turned to them with a look of bemusement. "The two of you?" He laughed. "You are my dear friends, but neither of you has what it takes to accomplish the theft of such a precious article."

"We don't?" Rufus asked, crossing his arms.

"No," Saif said. He took a few steps back toward them. "To make a gem such as the Chandramukhi your own requires planning and precision. It requires unscrupulous accomplices with secrets that can be used against them should they squeal. And for a diamond of renown, it requires connection with one with the ability to recut it into many smaller, though equally valuable, diamonds."

A shiver went down Felix's back and his nerves prickles. "You seem to know a great deal about the matter."

Saif shrugged. "What can I say. I was blessed with an imagination. But enough of unpleasant things." He clapped his hands together and closed the distance between them. "I have come to invite you to an evening of dancing and drink, of scintillating conversation and sinful company."

"Your father is hosting another party?" Rufus asked, his arms still crossed.

"Of course," Saif said. "But this one will be special. This one will be talked about for months to come."

"What is different about this one?" Felix asked.

Saif held his arms wide. "I will be there," he said, then added with an impish grin, "Don't tell me you haven't missed me."

Felix broke into a grin. "You do make your father's revels interesting," he admitted. Indeed, Saif always came up with some sort of game or activity for the party-goers to participate in that left everyone exceptionally drunk, ridiculously aroused, and rolling with laughter.

"It will be a night to remember," Saif went on. "The food will be sumptuous and the wine of the best quality. There will be gifts and surprises for all."

"Gifts?" Rufus asked. "Has your father suddenly turned generous?"

"No, but his son has recently come into money. The treat is all mine," Saif said.

Felix frowned. Saif wouldn't be so foolish as to steal a diamond and to use the profits from its sale—in whole or recut into several new diamonds—to host a party. He hadn't been there the night the diamond was stolen. Then again, hadn't he just said that a true diamond thief would need accomplices? Perhaps someone else in the house had physically stolen the diamond on Saif's orders. After all, if simply being present the night the diamond went missing was enough to make both Felix and Rufus suspects, not being there might have ruled out Saif when he was, in fact, guilty.

Saif threw his arms around Felix's and Rufus's shoulders once more. "Come on, my friends. These revels won't be worth their price if you do not come. Bring women, if you want. All are welcome."

A rush of desire filled Felix at the thought of bringing Josephine to the party. Would she be shocked by the kind of debauchery Khan's parties usually involved or would she embrace it? The tightening in his groin told him she'd embrace it. He might be tempted to embrace her as well in a particularly carnal way. He'd already tipped his cards where sensual activity was concerned, so why not throw caution to the wind and anticipate his wedding vows? His mother would be overjoyed if he petitioned her to speed the marriage along.

"When is this grand fete?" he asked.

"Friday night," Saif answered with a broad grin. "You are coming?"

Felix put on the most salacious smile he could with his skin crawling the way it was. He hadn't suspected Saif of stealing the Chandramukhi Diamond until that point, but now he couldn't shake the idea. But at the same time, the thought of enjoying Josephine at one of Khan's routs was irresistible.

"I'm coming," he said at last. He would sort out the rest later.

CHAPTER 5

"*I* tell you, it was like nothing I've seen before," Jo whispered to Caro the afternoon after her momentous tea with Lord Lichfield. "An entire cupboard filled with riding crops and flails and other baffling items."

"Hmm, I see," Caro replied, that sage look in her eyes that hinted to Jo that her friend knew far more than she commonly revealed. She flicked her paintbrush across the saucer she was painting, creating a clumsy flower, and added, "He does have a particular reputation, after all."

Jo finished off the daisy she'd been painting on her saucer, then swished her brush in the glass of water at her place in the workroom to clean it. "Believe me, I am now well acquainted with his reputation," she said, squirming uncomfortably in a seat that felt a hundred times harder than it had two days before. "My backside is more than aware."

Caro only barely managed to hide a snigger as Miss Dobson glanced across the room to them. She carried a switch that she tapped against her free hand as she spaced up and down the rows of toiling pupils, inspecting their work. Miss Dobson's eyes met Caro's and narrowed. She continued her menacing pacing, working her way up the row to Jo and Caro and making it impossible for the two of them to finish their conversation.

It had been the same since the moment Jo returned to the school after luncheon the day before. Jo had been bursting to tell Caro everything that had transpired between her and Lord Lichfield. She could hardly believe it had all happened to begin with. It all seemed like a dream. Indeed, it had seemed like a dream from the moment Lord Lichfield cleaned himself up after the explosion she had caused and calmly escorted her back down to his front parlor. His mother and hers had seemed only mildly irritated when Lord Lichfield explained that Jo had gotten lost on the way back from her unmentionable errand and had found herself in the library. His story was accepted without question, even when Jo winced as she resumed her seat on the couch. Lord Lichfield had noted her discomfort with a concealed grin and a glint in his eyes that promised Jo there would be far more where the first had come from once they were wed.

"Unacceptable," Miss Dobson hissed as she glanced over Jo and Caro's shoulders at their work. "Those saucers need to match the cups before you."

"Yes, miss," Jo and Caro answered in unison.

"Pay attention and do your work accurately," Miss Dobson went on, tapping each of their backs with her switch. Although "tap" was too gentle a word for what she did.

Jo swallowed and narrowed her eyes at the teacup she had been assigned to paint a corresponding saucer for. She didn't know how Miss Dobson expected them to duplicate someone else's work, but she insisted on marketing matched sets.

Jo concentrated so acutely on her painting out of fear of reprisal that she nearly didn't notice when Miss Dobson walked on, declaring, "Lady Eliza, that is the worst excuse for a rose I've seen all day."

With Eliza and Felicity the new object of Miss Dobson's irritation, Jo and Caro were able to breathe easier.

"Nipple clamps," Caro whispered at last.

"What?" Jo answered too loudly, jerking straight so fast that she smeared paint across her saucer.

She was forced to reach for a cloth to rub it away before the paint dried as Miss Dobson snapped back to face her. Blessedly, Felicity chose precisely that moment to knock her glass of brush-cleaning water over, thus drawing Miss Dobson's attention. Jo reminded herself to find a way to thank Felicity and Eliza.

"What?" she whispered to Caro, though her shock was no less acute.

"The necklace you thought you found," Caro

murmured. "The attachments are intended to be firmly fastened around one's nipples. Tightly fastened."

Jo gaped at her. "Wouldn't that hurt?" she asked, absently rubbing the front of her uniform.

"That's precisely the point," Caro whispered in return. "It's a form of sexual play that has become very popular since the publication of works by the Marquis de Sade."

"But...." Jo scrambled for words and shook her head. "Isn't that precisely the opposite point of—" she glanced over her shoulder to be sure Miss Dobson was nowhere near, "—those activities?"

Caro shrugged. "Some people believe that you first must experience pain before you can arrive at pleasure."

Jo blinked. "Do you believe that?"

"Heavens no," Caro laughed.

"Ladies," Miss Dobson shouted from the other end of the room. "Must I remind you that this is a time for silent work and contemplation?"

"Yes, Miss Dobson," the two long tables of pupils intoned in unison.

Jo glanced around, realizing that she and Caro hadn't been the only ones whispering and giggling. Miss Dobson looked excessively put out about the whole thing. Instead of making another round through the tables, she sank into a chair near the window at the front of the room and stared out with wistful eyes.

Jo attempted to concentrate on her painting, but her mind had chosen to run riot, replaying the scene from

Lord Lichfield's bedroom the day before. It had hurt to be spanked like a child—her bottom and her pride. And yet, the pain had given way to pleasure. Pleasure of an intensity that she had never known. If she was honest, it had been a pleasure of a different sort to unman Lord Lichfield as payment for his mischievousness. Perhaps there was some merit to the idea of beginning with discomfort to reach ecstasy.

"I will tell you one thing," she resumed speaking her thoughts aloud as she and Caro pretended to focus on their work.

Caro raised an eyebrow and peeked sideways at her in question.

"I am more certain than ever that Lord Lichfield is the diamond thief," Jo finished.

Caro turned fully toward her. "Last night you were certain he couldn't be."

Jo nibbled on her lip, feeling sheepish for having changed her mind. "If he enjoys inflicting pain on women, it stands to reason that he is a blackguard. Therefore, would it not follow that he stole the diamond?"

Caro chuckled gently, shaking her head. "If your Lord Lichfield is what I think he is, the women upon whom he inflicts pain invite and enjoy the process."

"But again," Jo said, "why would any woman—"

Her question was cut short as Miss Dobson leapt up from her chair with a gasp. She continued to look out the window. In fact, she threw open the glass, sending a burst of chilled air into the room, and leaned out. She waved silently at someone, hissing as if attempting to snag their attention. Apparently, her efforts failed. She jerked back into the room, slammed the window shut, then turned and rushed for the door.

"Continue with your painting, ladies. Miss Cade, you are in charge," she called out before vanishing around the corner into the hall.

Miss Cade had all of five seconds before her smug grin fell into a look of dread. No sooner had Miss Dobson left the room than Felicity and Eliza rose from their seats.

"Well, well, Miss Cade," Felicity said. "Are you in charge?" She drew a length of cord from the pocket concealed in her skirt.

"No," Miss Cade gasped. "You wouldn't."

But Felicity and Eliza would. Miss Cade tried to run, but she had no allies. Within a minute, Felicity and Eliza had captured her, bound her hands behind her, tied a gag around her mouth, and began painting flowers and woodland creatures on her face. The workroom descended into complete disorder as the pent-up pupils released energy that had been stifled for too long. It was utter, delightful madness.

"Hurry," Caro said, rising from her seat and stepping over the bench. "She obviously snuck out to speak with someone. If we catch her saying something untoward, we will have fuel to bring her before a magistrate for abuse."

"You're right."

Jo jumped up from her seat as well. As their fellow inmates expended their energy throwing paint around and breaking teacups and saucers, Jo and Caro rushed to the window. They were just in time to see Miss Dobson disappear into the house owned by the East India Company.

"This is too brilliant," Caro said with a laugh. "We can catch her in the midst of a scandalous assignation."

"Or worse," Jo said, giggling with glee.

The two of them hurried from the workroom and tore up the stairs to their bedroom. It was harder to push the wardrobe out of the way without Rebecca's help, but they managed it. Then, each carrying a candle, they slipped into the secret passageway between the school and the East India Company house.

"Where do you think she's gone?" Jo asked as they started along the passageway to the set of impossibly narrow stairs that led one floor down. In the weeks since Rebecca's departure and subsequent marriage, Jo and Caro had explored the passages fully and were now well-versed in every room and hallway they could observe through peepholes.

"She hasn't had time to sequester herself and whoever she rushed to meet in any of the upper rooms," Caro said.

"Then we continue to head down," Jo whispered.

Even in the middle of the afternoon, the East India Company's house was active. It wasn't simply a location for scandalous revels, after all. Jo had listened in on quite a few meetings of investors and potential governors on their way to and from the subcontinent. In her eavesdropping, she had learned that a man could become ridiculously wealthy through bribes and underhanded dealings in the subcontinent. She'd learned that the East India Company was actively engaged in pitting rajas of the various regions against each other and against the Mughal emperor for their own gain. And she'd discovered that even though the British businessmen and hired officers didn't think highly of the native Indians, those Indians were intelligent, determined, and filled with pride in their homeland. In Jo's opinion, if the East India Company didn't adjust many of its practices, it would encounter trouble in the future.

Those thoughts were sharp in her mind as she turned a corner and heard the unmistakable sound of a man and a woman enjoying each other. What snagged her attention was that the man spoke in one of the many Indian languages she'd heard spoken in the house, but the woman responded in English.

"Good heavens," she gasped, stopping beside the room where the activity was taking place.

"What is it?" Caro hissed.

Jo touched a finger to her lips and gestured for Caro to come take her candle. They'd learned that there was far less likelihood of the peepholes that peered into the rooms being discovered if no light escaped through.

Once Caro had her candle, Jo silently slipped the peephole's covering open. As expected, the first thing Jo spotted was the man and woman entwined in passion on a round bed. There was nothing particularly exceptional about their coupling other than the fact that the Indian man was young and handsome, and in all of the spying she had done in the past few weeks, Jo had never seen him before. The woman was one of the English prostitutes who had discovered there was a great deal of money to be made at the house.

What caught Jo's eye were the clothes draped over a chair immediately next to where the peephole was located. The Indian man's clothes were of western design, and quite expensive by the looks of them. His Hessian boots were of the finest quality and stood upright beside the chair. But along with the fine clothing, a variety of coins, ticket stubs, and bits of paper were scattered across the seat of the chair as though they'd fallen out of a pocket. Jo was just close enough to read the scraps of paper.

Her eyes popped wide, and she stifled a gasp. One of the scraps bore an address in Fitzrovia along with a scribbled note that read, "Lichfield's den of love."

Jo slid the peephole closed as fast as she could with her blood suddenly pumping furiously through her. She repeated the Fitzrovia address several times, quickly, committing it to memory. Lichfield's den of love. Lord Lichfield must have owned a separate property in London. And it stood to reason that if he had a massive, precious diamond to hide, he would hide it at an address far from where he lived, an address few people knew he had.

"What is it?" Caro whispered when Jo scurried over to her and took her candle.

"Lichfield's den of love," Jo whispered in return.

In the candlelight, Caro's brow shot up. "Lichfield? In there? Speaking Hindi?"

"No, no." Jo shook her head. "I don't know who that was. He appears to be handsome, though."

"Oh?" Caro glanced back over Jo's shoulder as though tempted to go see for herself.

Jo pushed her on, silently reminding her of why they were there. "The important thing is that Lord Lichfield has a second address. A second address where he could be concealing the diamond."

"If he is, indeed, the thief," Caro added.

"I'm as sure now as I ever was," Jo said. Although, admittedly, that wasn't as certain as she needed to be. But with the information she'd just discovered, she now had a way to investigate further.

Caro answered with an uncertain look, but before they could discuss the matter further, the unmistakable sound of Miss Dobson's voice drifted through the wall on the other side of the passageway. Caro and Jo both made signs for the other to be silent before they inched closer to the wall.

"I tell you, I have a buyer for you," Miss Dobson said.

"Madam, keep your voice down," a man's voice said. It sounded vaguely familiar to Jo.

"But you said time is of the essence." Miss Dobson's voice grew closer to the wall. "I have a buyer who is inter-

ested in the diamond, but the sale must take place immediately."

Jo searched frantically for a peephole she could slide
open, but there were none on that side of the wall. The
room where Miss Dobson and the man spoke must have
been one of the larger, public rooms or a hallway and not
a room designed for a rendezvous.

"What buyer?" the man asked, clearly only a few
inches away from where Jo and Caro leaned in, on the
other side of the wall.

"A contact of my father's." Miss Dobson lowered her
voice to a whisper, but she was still clearly audible to Jo
and Caro. "He's as rich as Croesus and as unscrupulous
as Herod. He wants the diamond for his private collection." She paused. "You would be surprised at what he
holds in that collection."

"No doubt," the man muttered. "But would he be
able to pay what I'm asking?"

"Able?" Miss Dobson scoffed. "He could buy the
Palace of Versailles if he chose to."

The man made an appreciative, avaricious sound.
"Tell him I'll speak to him," he said.

"When? Where?" Miss Dobson asked.

"Here," the man said. "Khan's prodigal son has
returned, and the whelp will be hosting a particularly
large, wicked bacchanal here on Friday."

"Are you certain it's safe here?" Miss Dobson asked.
"What if someone sees the diamond?"

The man chuckled. "My dear girl, I would never

show the diamond here. No, no, it is safe where it is, in the hands of a friend."

Jo pressed her free hand to her chest. Lord Lichfield. It had to be. Perhaps he did not steal the diamond himself, but he could be an accomplice. After all, not five minutes before, she had discovered he owned property no one knew about. Everything seemed to fit together perfectly to paint a dastardly picture.

"My father's contact will want to see the diamond," Miss Dobson went on. "He will want proof that you can deliver what you say you can."

"Tell him not to worry," the man said. "Tell him that I will bring what he requires to the revels on Friday night."

"I will," Miss Dobson said, then added, "My sweet."

A disgusting, squelchy noise followed, along with a gasp and moan from Miss Dobson. Jo reeled back from the wall, a look of revulsion on her face. Caro wore a matching look. They'd heard everything they needed to hear, and the time seemed ideal to beat a hasty retreat. Miss Dobson would be returning to the school in a matter of minutes, in all likelihood, which meant that Felicity and Eliza would need a good and proper warning that their reign of terror needed to end post haste.

But once they returned to their room and were sliding the wardrobe back into place, Jo said, "I'm going in search of the diamond."

"You are?" Caro blinked at her, seemingly impressed. "But where? How?"

"It's at Lord Lichfield's secret address, obviously," Jo said.

The wardrobe thumped back into place and Caro straightened, planting her hands on her waist. "Are you certain you do not wish to investigate Lord Lichfield's secret address for the purpose of repeating your activities of yesterday?"

Jo's face heated. "And if I did, what would you have to say about it?"

Caro broke into a grin. "I'd say that you must enjoy yourself thoroughly and report back to me in detail every-thing that transpires."

"You wouldn't think I am a scandalous hussy for anticipating my wedding vows?"

"Heavens, no," Caro laughed. "I would do the same, if given half a chance."

Jo laughed along with her, but she couldn't shake the feeling that Caro might land herself in quite a bit of trouble someday, likely someday soon.

CHAPTER 6

It was as Jo was zipping across Oxford Street and up a quiet street in Fitzrovia the next day, the maid Flora accompanying her as chaperone, that Jo decided Felicity Murdoch and Lady Eliza Towers were geniuses. Not only had they managed to avoid blame for the chaos that Miss Dobson returned to after her illicit meeting at the house owned by the East India Company—although all of the young ladies of the school had been punished by being sent to bed without supper— as soon as Jo explained her need to escape from the school for a day, they went right to work without asking questions.

They managed to lace Miss Dobson's morning coffee with a tincture of opium. The result was that Miss Dobson excused herself at the end of breakfast so that she could lie down. The moment she was sound asleep, Felicity and Eliza had locked Miss Cade, Miss Conyer, and Miss Warren in the attic, and the pupils had bliss-fully declared a holiday, fleeing the school in every direction.

Jo had expected Caro to come with her, but Caro had declared she had a different sort of errand to run, which left Jo in the unsatisfactory company of Flora.

"This is a bad idea, miss," Flora said in foreboding tones as the hired hack rocked to a stop in front of the address Jo remembered as Lord Lichfield's secret residence. "What if no one is home?"

"I'm counting on that," Jo said as they alighted from the carriage. She paid the driver, then crept up to one of the front windows as Flora watched the hack depart with a nervous expression.

"How are we going to get home, miss?" Flora asked.

"If we have to, we'll walk down to Oxford Street. I'm certain we can hire a hack there," Jo answered, barely paying attention to the maid.

She cupped her hands to the sides of her eyes and peered into the house. There was nothing unusual about it, except, perhaps, that the curtains were parted enough for her to see inside. All she spied was a plain, rather small parlor with middle-class decorations. When she skipped around to the window on the other side of the front door, all she saw was an uninteresting dining room. If she hadn't known better, she would have assumed the house belonged to a clerk's family. But as long as she studied the house's interior, she saw no one moving about

—not a housewife nor a maid nor anyone who might live there.

"This is certainly the house," she said, mostly to herself, stepping back to study the building. "Now, how do we get in?"

"I'm not going in there, miss," Flora said, shaking her head adamantly. "I'm no housebreaker."

"We aren't stealing anything," Jo told her. They were there to recover something that had been stolen, but she hadn't told Flora any of that. "Perhaps we would do best to enter through the downstairs," she said, heading for the alley between Lord Lichfield's house and the next.

Jo counted herself lucky that the path leading to the kitchen door was clear and open. A maid was busy scrubbing pots in the garden in back of the neighboring house, but a brick wall served to conceal Jo's activity as she tested the kitchen door and then the windows.

At last, she found a window that wasn't latched and that swung open when she pushed on it. "This is our way in," she whispered to Flora, dragging a crate that had been left in the garden over to the window. "I'll slip in and unlock the door and you can—"

"No, miss," Flora said, shaking her head and backing up. "I won't do it. I'm not a bad girl, like the lot of you. I won't do it." Her words dissolved into a veil of tears, and as she finished, she turned and fled.

Jo let out an irritated breath. She should have tried harder to convince Caro to come with her. Still, it wasn't a huge misfortune that she would have to go on alone. She could be quicker and quieter on her own.

With renewed confidence, she climbed up on the crate and pushed the kitchen window open. It was more of a trial to climb through than she would have imagined. Her efforts ended up including a fair amount of grunting and flailing. When at last she squeezed through the window, the drop she experienced was greater than she anticipated. With a yelp, she spilled to the floor, failing to catch herself in time and landing hard on her backside.

"I'm not certain I appreciate the irony," she said as she stood, rubbing her poor, bruised bottom. It seemed even Lord Lichfield's secret address had curious tendencies toward abuse.

She put the thought aside and crept slowly through the kitchen toward a hallway that she assumed led to the rest of the house.

"If I were hiding a priceless diamond, where would I put it," she whispered.

The answer was as obvious then as it had been the day she'd gone to Lord Lichfield's proper house with her mother for tea. Something as precious as a diamond would be kept in the innermost, most intimate room in the house. Which meant that all she needed to do was to locate Lord Lichfield's bedroom.

She made her way up to the first floor, craning her neck to look inside each room as she passed. The front rooms were mostly empty, which immediately ruled them out as potential diamond repositories.

In retrospect, she should have realized that the quiet, shuffling sounds she heard as she made her way to the back of the house to check those rooms were portents of disaster. As it was, she didn't think about them until she was in the midst of pushing open a half-closed door at the far end of the short hall. Hers wasn't the only gasp of surprise as she stepped incautiously into the room and found herself face to face with Lord Lichfield.

The two of them stood gaping at each other for a moment. Shock left Jo immobilized. The room was indeed a bedchamber, though it was decorated far more simply than Lord Lichfield's room in his proper house. It held little more than a simple bed covered with a quilt, a plain wardrobe—which stood open and was mostly empty—and a dusty washstand in the corner. A trunk stood open on the chest at the foot of the bed. Lord Lichfield looked as though he were either unpacking and moving things into the wardrobe or packing up what had been inside. He was in his shirtsleeves without a cravat, and he held a robe of red, Chinese silk in one hand and what appeared to be a medieval flail in the other.

Jo's observations happened in a moment, and as soon as sense rushed back to her, she asked, "What are you doing here?"

Lord Lichfield uttered the exact same words at the same time, then answered with, "This is my house."

Jo's face heated, and twin snakes of embarrassment and excitement twined through her gut. There would be no looking for the diamond now. Although it seemed painfully obvious to her that it must be nearby, in the very room where they stood, perhaps. She'd come all this way, risked a great deal to prove his guilt. Now was not the time to back down. Besides, she couldn't have found another excuse for her presence in his secret house on such short notice.

So she squared her shoulders, tilted her chin up, and said, "The game is over, Lord Lichfield. I know all about your notorious doings."

Surprise flashed across his face for a moment before his expression turned sly and tempting. He tossed the robe and the crop into the chest, then stepped around to face Jo more fully. "I haven't doubted for a moment that you knew all of my secrets." He stepped closer, his presence growing intimidating. "That's why you sought me out the other day, isn't it?"

Jo's whole body heated at the mention of the other day. The same core of liquid fire that he'd ignited in her sex then flared back to life. But she couldn't stray from her mission.

"I'm surprised you admit your guilt, my lord," she said, forcing her body not to tremble as he moved close enough for her to catch his delicious scent.

For a moment, Lord Lichfield's wolfish expression dipped into a confused frown. "I would hardly call it guilt. Concupiscence, perhaps."

It was Jo's turn to frown in confusion. "Concupiscence?" She blinked. "What does concupiscence have to do with being a diamond thief?"

Lord Lichfield's eyes went wide and his expression flashed from confusion to amusement for a moment before the mask of virility he'd worn returned. "You think I am a diamond thief?"

Jo was no longer so certain, but she dropped her shoulders, blew out a breath, and said, "Well, aren't you?"

Rather than answering her directly, he crossed his arms and glanced down his nose at her. "Do you actually believe me capable of theft?"

"You are quite capable of other things," she said, a hitch forming in her voice as her memory conjured up what all those things were. The bruise she'd suffered breaking into the house only accentuated her memories.

He continued to stare at her with a mixture of incredulity and attempted intimidation. Jo had the feeling his efforts to exert mastery over her were, in fact, merely an attempt and that other emotions were busy superseding what she was beginning to suspect was an act. She decided to jump in before he recovered his bearings.

"You were at the East India Company's house on the day the Chandramukhi Diamond was stolen, weren't you?" she asked, remembering the way she'd seen Rebecca's Nigel ask questions.

"Yes," he answered slowly and in a low voice, his eyes narrowed as though he were reading her.

"And you own a secret property, unbeknownst to most of society," she went on, gesturing around the room.

His lips twitched and his eyes flashed with amusement. "I can assure you, the purpose of this townhouse is not housing stolen goods."

"It is obviously intended for some nefarious use," Jo said, feeling less and less certain about her assumptions with each second that ticked by.

"Yes," he admitted, taking a step forward. "It is. And do you want to know what purpose that is?"

"It's not for hiding diamonds?" she asked, her voice turning small and uncertain.

"No."

He stepped so close to her that she was forced to backpedal. At least until she thumped up against the wall. Lord Lichfield didn't stop there, though. He grabbed her hands and pinned them to the wall above her head, similarly to the way he had wedged her against the door to his closet the other day. Jo's breath came in shallow gulps as her legs turned to melted butter and her sex throbbed. He couldn't possibly mean to repeat their activities of the other day, could he?

"I recently purchased this house from a friend," he said in a low voice against her ear. "I purchased it for the purpose of luring naughty young women inside. Cheeky little minxes who housebreak and accuse their fiancés of stealing."

"Did you really?" she asked, her voice quivering with a mixture of fear and lust.

"No," he answered, his tone surprisingly forthright. He leaned back a bit, still pinning her wrists against the wall. There was a curious earnestness in his eyes as he studied her. "I purchased it from a friend in financial straits as a means of helping him out."

"Lord Herrington?" Jo asked, attempting to fit the pieces of things she'd overheard together.

Lord Lichfield frowned slightly. "How did you know?"

"I...I know Lord Herrington is in financial difficulty," Jo confessed. "It is widely known."

Concern painted Lord Lichfield's expression. "Rufus won't be happy about that."

Of all things, a pulse of tenderness filled Jo's heart. Lord Lichfield must have cared considerably for his friend to be so concerned about his feelings. Knowing that made the heat growing within her spike.

A second later, the rakish mask Lord Lichfield wore snapped back into place. He pressed his hips against hers. Jo sucked in a breath at the hard bulge that ground against her.

"I purchased this place as a den where I can entertain women in need of strict discipline," he said.

Jo's eyebrows lifted in shock. A moment later, they angled into a scowl. He was supposed to marry her, and yet he intended to consort with women? Women like the ones she'd spied through the walls of the East India Company's house who seemed to enjoy being punished?

Before she could take him to task for infidelity, Lord Lichfield said, "I purchased it for that reason, but now I have no intention of using it that way."

Jo blinked. "You don't?"

"No," he said. "There is only one woman I know of now who deserves a damn good thrashing for her insolence."

In a flash, Jo's scowl was back as she contemplated who that woman could be. It was only when he yanked her away from the wall, spun her around, and pressed her into the wall chest first while he tugged at the ties of her gown that Jo realized he meant her.

"Cheeky minxes who accuse their future husbands of stealing diamonds need to be punished," he said, finishing with the ties of her gown and pushing the bodice roughly down over her shoulders. "Wicked young ladies who housebreak will most certainly pay the price."

He tugged her back against his chest and continued undressing her with demanding movements. He untied her petticoat and shoved it and her gown over her hips so that they dropped to the floor, then went to work on her stays. When they fell away, he closed his hands around her breasts and kneaded them forcefully.

"Oh," Jo sighed, closing her eyes and resting her head back against his shoulder. "Oh, my." She arched her back, thrusting her breasts more fully into his hands.

The pressure with which Lord Lichfield handled her eased a bit. "Do you like that?" he asked, a note of genuine curiosity in his voice.

"I like the way you touch me, but perhaps not so hard," she said before she thought better about criticizing him.

For the briefest of moments, he was perfectly still.

When he resumed teasing and caressing her breasts, it was with a far gentler touch. "Like this?" he asked.

A shudder of pleasure swept through her, tightening her sex, especially when he began teasing her nipples into sensitive nubs. "Yes," she sighed, wriggling her hips against his.

He sucked in a breath, jerking his hips away for a moment before grinding his hardening staff against her backside. Jo couldn't believe the heaven she'd fallen into. At least she couldn't until he pinched both of her nipples hard.

"Ow!" She wrenched away from him, twisting to face him with a scowl. She had half a mind to slap his face and only just held back. "That wasn't very nice," she said, hugging herself.

He stared back at her with more confusion than lust, though the lust was certainly there. It grew when his gaze dropped to her torso. Jo was suddenly aware that she stood before him in nothing but an extremely thin chemise that hid very little from his view. Her pulse sped up as she embraced the deliciousness of being exposed to him that way.

"I'll let you take my chemise off if you promise to be nice to me," she said, her heart beating like a drum against her ribs. It felt sinfully good to tempt him that way.

Judging by the size of the bulge in his breeches, he was sorely tempted. "You'll remove your chemise if I tell you to remove it, you wicked little harlot."

Jo's eyes popped wide in indignation. "You would call your future wife a name like that?"

"If she deserves it," he said.

There was something challenging in his eyes, something bright and full of fire. She'd seen plenty of men who were truly cruel and heartless, who would have called her names and spoken meanly to her. Her heart told her Lord Lichfield wasn't one of those men. The things he said were a game, and she wanted to win.

"If I am a harlot, then you are a...a jackal." Inwardly Jo winced, wishing she knew more vulgar names for a man of loose morals. "I won't budge an inch from this spot or take off my chemise unless you remove all of your clothes."

Fire danced in his eyes. "Do you think that is a threat, minx?" he asked, unbuttoning and shrugging out of his waistcoat before tossing it aside. "I'll show you a threat."

Jo instantly wondered if her gamble was a wise one as he peeled his shirt off over his head, revealing the broad, muscular expanse of his chest with its dark hair. He bent over to pull off his boots—which took more effort than she would have imagined. So much so that the tension of the moment was almost shattered. It was recovered a moment later when he straightened and undid the fall of his breeches while staring straight at her eyes.

At last, he shoved his breeches down over his hips with a defiant gesture. Jo's eyes dropped from his to the magnificent length of his penis as it sprung up. It was thick and hard and the tip was fully flared. She'd seen

76

and indeed touched it the other day, but the full sight of him—his narrow hips, the dark hair at the base of his staff, the tight sacks of his testicles, as well as his fully engorged penis—was enough to leave Jo panting in expectation.

"Now," he said in a commanding voice, his eyes burning with lust. "Remove that chemise and brace yourself against my bed to receive your punishment."

Jo's mouth opened, but she couldn't think of a thing to say. She studied him, chewing her lip, trying to determine whether he was serious. And if he was serious, what did he intend to do with her? Her education at the East India Company's house caused several suggestions to spring to mind. All of them ended with her being impaled by his enormous manhood, though. If she did as he asked, she wouldn't leave the room with her virtue intact.

That thought propelled her forward. Cheeks blazing hot, sex throbbing, and morals crumbling around her, she pulled her chemise up over her head and tossed it aside before reaching his bed.

"H-how do you want me?" she asked, trembling from head to foot.

"Face the bed," he said. "Legs apart. Bend forward."

She did as he asked, her heart in her throat. The result was that she stood with her naked backside boldly presented to him as she braced her arms on the bed. She gasped when he came to stand directly behind her and thrust his hips against hers. She squeezed her eyes shut, waiting for the pain of penetration, but instead he merely teased her by stroking the wet folds of her sex with his cock. The sensation was strange but wonderful, especially when he angled himself to rub against her clitoris. Within seconds, she was wriggling against his movements, attempting to guide him to her entrance.

"Stay still," he ordered, bending over her to close her body in the cage of his own. "We've a long way to go before I give you what you want."

"It's what you want too," she told him over her shoulder.

She didn't know what made her say something so bold, but the result was captivating. He tensed against her, his hips thrusting as if on their own. She could feel his breath in short pants against her neck. He kept his hips pinned against hers, his penis tight between her legs, as he stroked her sides. His hands found her breasts and squeezed them, working her already sensitive nipples until her whole body felt as though it would burst into flame.

His hands moved to pull the pins from her hair. He tossed them aside, running his fingers through her locks to loosen her hair around her shoulders.

"I love the color of your hair," he hummed against her ear. "Auburn, like a sunset at sea."

His hands raked across her back and around to her sides and breasts again. His hips were still pinned firmly against hers, leaving Jo feeling strangely helpless. There were so many carnal things he could do to her in that position, things she wouldn't have been able to stop him from doing.

"What do you want?" he asked, his voice taking on a hard edge. "Do you want straps? Do you want to be lashed to the bed? Tied up? Do you want the spreader bar? Clamps? Should I use my hands or would you prefer a flail or the riding crop? I have a whip, but I can't guarantee my skill with it at this time."

The desire that had been building so steadily in Jo withered. "Is that what you think I want?" she asked breathlessly, glancing over her shoulder as best she could.

She could just barely see his face in the corner of his vision, but it was enough to see the confused, almost tortured look that entered his eyes.

"Isn't that why you're really here?" he asked. "Surely the diamond thing is just a ruse. You've heard about my skills and have come to test them for yourself."

Jo shook her head slightly. "What skills?"

"Lord Lichfield," he said, a certain harshness in his tone. "He can make you cry and come harder than you ever have at the same time." He sounded as though he was quoting someone else. "He can raise welts on your backside and make you beg for more. He is a demon lover who will spoil you for other men even as he robs you of the ability to sit for a week."

Jo frowned and shook her head. "I don't want any of that," she said.

He let out a frustrated breath and jerked away from her. Jo twisted to lie on her back only to see him shoving a hand through his hair. Something had upset him, but as much as she scrambled to think, she couldn't figure out what it was.

"What do you want from me?" he demanded, agitated. "What will you take this time?"

Jo was in the most indefensible position possible, both physically and morally. She lay splayed and naked on his bed, an intruder who had been thrust on him by his mother and her own silly ideas about diamond thieves. But at that moment, her heart understood things that her head could only wonder at.

"You," she said, uncertain where her courage or her emotion came from. "I just want you."

He went very still, his eyes wide as he studied her. The pain and frustration in his expression changed slowly to a different kind of hurt and a vulnerability that was so intimate she thought she should look away. But no, for better or for worse, the man in front of her would be her husband. She would treat him as such, starting immediately.

Tension filled his expression once more, and he surged back onto the bed, covering her body with his and pinning her arms at her sides. "Is this truly what you want?" he asked. "A seedy, used up rake who hurts women for pleasure?"

"You haven't hurt me," she said in a small voice. Immediately, she blushed and looked guilty. "Well, perhaps a bit the other day. But I had my share of fun as well."

He looked down at her as though she were something incomprehensible. Then, without further warning, he slanted his mouth over hers in a kiss. It wasn't the rough, punishing kiss she expected either. It was insistent, almost desperate, and deep. He parted her lips with his tongue then slipped in to explore her. His body took on an entirely different sort of tension as he pressed over her. Instead of the jagged tightness of anger, his body was warm and taut with desire.

She closed her arms around him, opening her hips and lifting one knee so that he could rest deeper in the cradle of her body. She brushed her hands across his back, sliding one hand up to thread through his hair. All the while, he kissed her, a deep rumble of pleasure sounding from low in his throat. The sound sent spirals of need through her, relighting the flames that his frustration had almost doused.

He raked one hand down her side while balancing with his other arm. He brushed the side of her breast before reaching lower. For a moment, Jo had the impression he wanted to reach between them, to stroke her sex the way he had before, but their bodies were twined together and she wasn't willing to give up the feeling of his flesh fully against hers.

At last, he broke away from her mouth, leaving her fluid and ready. He gazed down at her, brushing a lock of her hair off her cheek. "My God," he murmured. "You're beautiful."

Jo didn't know what to say. Her body ached for him.

She felt completely sensual and utterly at his mercy. His hot staff pressed against her inner thigh, and all she wanted was for him to be inside of her. She was certain that need was painted in every line of her face and that she looked as hungry for him as the most common courtesan.

"I have only one more thing to ask you," he said, sliding his hips against hers and stroking her with his length once more. He kissed her cheek, her neck, nibbled her earlobe. He lifted enough to close a hand fully over one of her breasts, teasing her nipple with his thumb.

"Ask," she sighed, unable to form more words than that.

"We're not married yet," he said, bending down to lick her pulse, then her lips. "Do you want me to spend in the sheets to protect you or do you want me to come inside you."

The question alone sent Jo so close to the edge of orgasm that she felt as though she might go mad. "Inside me," she panted, arching her hips against him. "Always inside me."

He groaned victoriously in response, then rocked back. When he surged forward once more it was not teasing or tempting. He guided himself to her entrance and pushed in, fast and hard, lodging himself deep.

Jo gasped at the sharp pain his thrust caused. He felt too big for her, too impossibly thick. She tensed and made a quick sound of protest, but he stayed firmly within her. He caressed her as well, stroking her sides and making soft soothing sounds between kisses. And within a scant heartbeat, what started off as shocking and uncomfortable quickly turned arousing.

"You're inside of me," she gasped, flexing her hips and squeezing her inner muscles, just to be sure.

"I am," he said in a strained voice. "It feels divine."

Jo wasn't so sure it felt divine for her, until he started to move. His thrusts were slow and shallow at first, creating just enough friction to feel interesting. The pain subsided to a dull ache, which took on an entirely different nature. It spread through her, coiling the tension tighter and tighter inside of her. But it was the sounds he made, low, soft sounds of pleasure that came from somewhere deep within her, in time to his increasing thrusts. They swirled around her, sinking deep into her heart. He was enjoying her. She had the power to give him pleasure, even passively.

She began to make her own sounds of pleasure in time to his thrusts as her body prepared for release. Instead of feeling too big inside of her, the way he stretched and filled her became intimate and arousing. She dug her fingertips into his back as his thrusts took on a frantic pace. That wasn't enough, so she lowered her hands to his backside, pressing her nails into his flesh.

With a gasp, he tensed and groaned. Warmth filled her as her body crashed into orgasm a moment later. It was an entirely new feeling to come with him lodged deep within her, to milk his stiff length even as his tension began to ebb and his body to relax above hers. His final groan of pleasure was rich and sated. She kept her legs locked around him until her throbbing stopped. Then the two of them simply lay where they were, hot, sweating, and joined in a tangle of limbs. As Jo closed her eyes, a smile on her face, she thanked every bit of bad luck that had brought her and Lord Lichfield together.

elix lay on his back in bed, one arm tucked behind his head, resting on the pillow. A lazy smile pulled at the corners of his mouth. He couldn't have stopped it if he'd tried. Because he wasn't alone in bed long after the act was done, for a change. Josephine snoozed, tucked against his side, her cheek nestled against his shoulder and her hand splayed over his heart.

"I just want you."

Those words, said in such an innocent, artless way, would never leave his heart as long as he lived. There was absolutely no logical reason why Josephine should have said such a thing to him. They barely knew each other. She thought he'd stolen the Chandramukhi Diamond. She'd seen the accessories to his sins. Hellfire, she'd experienced his wickedness personally. Still, all she wanted was him. And she had wanted him. She'd been wet and feverish, and when he'd taken her, she rode out the loss of her virginity to come in dazzling style just as he spilled into her. That kind of reaction wasn't artifice. It wasn't particularly sane either. But it was real, of that he was certain beyond anything he'd ever known.

He would make certain they were married by the end of the week. His title could buy him a special license in the minimum amount of time. They didn't have to have a grand ceremony. As soon as the marriage was announced in *The Times*, he would send the word ringing through London that Lord Lichfield was permanently out of the game. There were dozens of doms ready to take his place, and none of the women who had wasted their time with him had given even a sliver of their hearts away to him anyhow. His presence in the dark corners of society wouldn't be missed.

Josephine stirred, stretching out of her nap in a way that caused her body to slide against his enticingly. His resting cock instantly snapped awake with her.

"Oh, dear," she said, tensing and attempting to sit. "What is the time?"

"It is time to tangle yourself in your future husband's embrace," Felix said, pulling her back down to the mattress with him. He rolled to his side, wedging his leg between hers and lifting her thigh over his hip. "I haven't finished loving you yet."

"You haven't?" she asked, blinking into a wide-eyed, awed stare.

"No," he told her, leaning in to kiss her soundly,

breaking the kiss only to add, "Not if you still think I'm a dastardly diamond thief."

He kissed her again before she could say anything. She sighed with a combination of enjoyment and surprise that had his cock hardening further. Her mouth was soft and pliable under his, and she let him plunder her with abandon. She couldn't have had much experience kissing, but already he could tell she was a fast learner. It was in her eagerness, the way she clearly enjoyed every liberty he took with her.

He had just closed one hand around her breast and was about to work her nipple into a peak before shifting to suckle it when she tensed and pulled back. His heart crashed to his feet in the fear that she'd changed her mind about being the minx he needed her to be.

"Is something wrong?" he asked, cursing himself for sounding so vulnerable.

Instead of answering him with words, she wriggled away from him and pushed back the covers to expose most of their naked bodies. Then she lifted inexplicably to her knees and grabbed hold of his hip. She pulled him until he was face down, ass up, and then she sighed in relief.

"No birthmark," she said, as happy as she was relieved, patting his right cheek.

Felix laughed, utterly baffled by her actions. "Were you hoping for some sort of mark?"

"No," she said, sounding exceptionally earnest. "But

now I know beyond a shadow of a doubt you are not the diamond thief."

Felix laughed harder, rolling back to his side and pulling her down so that her back fit against his chest. "How do you know?" He wedged his leg between her thighs again and resumed playing with her breast.

Josephine hummed and squirmed against him before answering. "The diamond thief has a birthmark of a half-moon on his bottom. Rebecca, Caro, and I saw it."

Felix tensed. "How? When? Why would the diamond thief show you his ass?"

"He didn't," she said, twisting to look at him over her shoulder as best she could. She opened her mouth, paused before saying anything, closed her mouth, thought for a moment, then tried again. "There are secret passageways running through the house owned by the East India Company. As it happens, there is an entrance to those passageways in the room I share with Caro and we used to share with Rebecca. We've spent quite a good deal of time in those passageways, observing the goings on in many of the rooms of the house."

A rush of dread flooded Felix. He knew damn well what went on in those rooms. Hell, he'd availed himself of the private spaces a time or two himself, and not that long ago. For all he knew, his sweet, innocent wife-to-be had witnessed him rutting with one or the other of Khan's party guests.

"Did you—"

"We saw the diamond thief," she rushed on, so fast—

and without looking at him—that it all but confirmed she'd seen him misbehaving. At least he hadn't done more than a quick slap and suck at any of Khan's entertainments for months now. "Well, Rebecca did. But she told us every detail. He was deeply engaged with a woman who we suspect was Miss Dobson," Josephine went on, adding a revolted sound to the end of her words.

"Not a sight I would care to see," Felix agreed, happy to move on from anything that would paint him in a bad light, much though he probably deserved it.

"We don't know for certain as the woman's gown concealed her upper half." Josephine twisted to face him again. "And the man was facing away from Rebecca. Which is how she had a distinct view of his bottom and its birthmark."

Felix could only imagine. "How do you know he was the thief?"

Josephine flushed and looked beautifully scandalized. "Apparently, he spoke about it. Rebecca swears he said that he should have—" she paused to giggle, "—should have inserted the diamond into the woman's cunny so that she could have simply walked out of the house without it being detected."

Felix smirked. "What a charming bit of vulgarity. It would have worked, though."

"Would it?" Josephine asked. "Wouldn't the diamond have slipped out?"

"Not if an effort was made to hold it within."

She seemed to contemplate that for a moment. Felix

took advantage of her silence to resume his intimate study of her body. He wanted to learn every inch of her, feel her body's response to his touch in every spot, so that he could figure out how best to pleasure her. In a way, it was like starting all over again. He'd spent so long with women who found their pleasure in pain that he had to relearn the purity of coupling for its own sake.

Her skin was deliciously soft, warm, and carried a uniquely feminine scent. When he was satisfied that her nipples would remain pebbled, at least for a while, he brushed his fingers down over her belly, eliciting a shiver from her.

"Ooh, that feels good," she gasped, wriggling her backside against him.

His cock twitched at the rush of sensation her movements gave him. It settled nicely into the cleft of her backside as it hardened even more.

"Does it?" he asked, lazy and teasing. "How about this?"

He delved into her curls, sinking his fingers into her folds and stroking what he found there. She let out a sound of pleasure and strained against him, but he didn't increase the intensity of his touch. He'd brought her to orgasm in a rush, after spanking her, and through penetration—which still surprised him. Now he wanted to lead her on a slow, heady journey to the most powerful orgasm she'd ever had.

Josephine, of course, had other plans.

"You're so good at this," she said, nearly squealed,

with pleasure. "Why would you ever choose to spank a woman to arouse her?"

He stopped, a cold shiver passing through him. An odd lump formed in his throat, and his heart beat harder with anxiety. "Would you like to know how it started?"

"Yes, please," she said, twisting once again to look over her shoulder at him.

He kept his hand firmly buried in her pussy, stroking softly as he explained. "It was an accident. I was—" he cleared his throat, "—visiting with a woman."

"A lover," Josephine said.

"I was young," he said in affirmation. "It's something most young noblemen with too much money and too little occupation do."

"Understood," she said, oddly without judgment.

"As I said," he continued, "I was with a woman, and I'm not precisely certain how it happened, but as we were both undressing, we collided in such a way that my hand made sharp contact with her backside."

Josephine arched an eyebrow at him doubtfully.

"I swear on my life, it was an accident," he said, raising one hand as if taking an oath. "I began to apologize, but the woman asked me to do it again. Then again." He sighed. "Before I knew it, I had her turned over my knee, her backside bright red, and all the while she squealed and cried 'Papa, I'll be good, I promise.'"

Josephine blinked. "Something about that doesn't sound quite right."

"It wasn't," he admitted. "But as I have since discovered, there are a great many women in the world—some you would never suspect—who harbor a visceral need to be punished and humiliated. To be honest, I don't understand it."

"You don't?" She twisted until she lay on her back and was better able to study his face.

He shrugged. "Not one bit."

"But it still arouses you," she said.

A pinch of guilt hit him. "I don't think my dominance or their humiliation is what arouses me."

"No? What then?"

His mouth twitched into a lopsided, somewhat sheepish grin. "Naked women. Wet, naked women. Knowing what's in it for me after they've climaxed."

Once again, she arched an eyebrow at him as if she didn't believe a word he said. "It must be more than that."

"I truly don't think it is," he argued.

"All right," she said, moving away from him and slipping out of bed. "Shall we put the theory to the test?"

His heart sped up at the mischief in her eyes. He scooted across the bed, throwing his legs around the side and standing. "What do you have in mind?" At that moment, he would have done anything Josephine told him to do.

Her grin turned downright wicked. "Face the bed. Legs apart. Bend forward," she said in a perfect imitation of the tone and force he'd used when he said the exact same words.

Damn him if her command didn't send the blood that had drifted away while they talked right back to his cock. He eyed her cagily, but slowly moved to do as she said. He moved his feet apart and leaned forward, propping his arms on the bed and presenting his ass to her. His cock ached as it hung slightly away from his body, hard and heavy.

"Let's see," Josephine said impishly as she crossed behind him. "How best to go about the test."

"You don't have the black streak within you that is necessary for this sort of play," he told her as she reached the foot of the bed.

"Don't I?" She met his eyes challengingly before reaching into the trunk where he'd been packing away his toys and drew out the riding crop.

His groin tightened in a response that shocked him with its strength. A strange sense of shame followed hard on its heels. Instead of feeling distaste or nothing at all, he caught himself wondering if she could strike him hard enough to make a difference.

The uncomfortable feeling of shame intensified when she lashed out, cracking the leather of the crop across his ass with only a mild sting. Shame because he'd wanted it to hurt much more than it had.

"See, you don't have what it takes," he said, purposefully contemptuous. "You're far too sweet and ignorant to—"

She struck him harder—hard enough for him to lose his train of thought. The sting of the blow remained, even as she tilted to the side in an attempt to get a look at his face.

"You aren't going to be able to—"

She smacked him again, hard enough for his whole body to flinch. And then again with a force that made him so hard he felt he was in danger of coming across the coverlet. But he deserved it. He could feel it in his deepest core. He deserved to be punished for all the horrible things he'd done to all the women who had sought him out over the years. He deserved to get what he'd given. Even more than that, he deserved every bit of the complicated clash of arousal and shame that clawed at him. It wasn't just the pain of the blow—and he cried out with far too much pleasure at her next, sharp swat—that he deserved to feel to the marrow of his bones, it was the emotional agony of harboring something dark and conflicted within him. Maybe, if he could feel the inner pain physically, he could release it and be free of it forever.

Josephine brought the riding crop down with what felt like her full strength, sending searing pain through his ass. At the same time, the impossibly tight ball of energy that had built behind his balls began to surge.

"Oh, God," he gasped. "I'm coming."

"Oh," Josephine gasped. She moved quickly, rushing forward and under him to close her free hand around his aching cock.

Felix had no idea if she thought she could stop his orgasm by holding him or if she was trying to speed the process, but within moments of her taking him in her hand, a thick stream of cum shot out of him. He let out a cry, thrusting against her a few times more before his body gave up, completely spent. All of the bad, all of the darkness, had spewed out of him, leaving him freer, lighter, purer.

He collapsed to the side, rolling to his back, panting. Josephine tossed the riding crop aside and sat on the bed beside him, rubbing his arm and studying his face.

"So?" she asked, an impossibly hopeful look in her eyes.

His ass was sore and his pride was wounded, but he was certain that both injuries would heal. "Insight," he managed to puff out as he caught his breath.

"I see," she said, arching that cheeky eyebrow of hers.

Deep affection filled his heart, and he gathered the strength he would need to make a move. "And you?" he asked. "Were you aroused by administering discipline?"

"Um," she tilted her head up, sending a look of false innocence up to the ceiling.

Felix didn't wait for her to go on. He lifted himself enough to hook an arm around her waist and to pull her down and across him. She yelped at the suddenness of his movements and when he pinned her on her back. He didn't have it in him to fuck her the way she deserved, but that didn't stop him from giving her what she needed. He rolled off the bed and onto his knees on the floor, pulling her with him. Her pussy was at the perfect height, and he gripped her knees, holding them slightly wider than he thought would be comfortable for her.

"Look at that," he said teasingly. "I haven't seen a quim so pink and wet in years."

"Lord Lichfield," she pleaded, half laughing.

"Felix," he told her. "You'll call me Felix from now on."

"Felix," she repeated.

"You wouldn't be so wet if whipping me hadn't given you pleasure," he said, leaning slowly closer to her pussy.

"It was rather invigorating," she said. Or at least that's what he assumed she would have said. He only let her get as far as, "It was rather invig—oh!"

The moment he brought his mouth to her folds and licked her slit deeply, he knew she wouldn't be able to hold out any longer than he had. She was already quivering and on the edge. All it would take was a few quick flickers across her clitoris and she would be gone. So, of course, he drew it out as long as he possibly could. He tasted her and kissed her, giving her a glimpse of where he might go next only to nibble at her inner thigh. She was panting and mewling with need in no time, grabbing fistfuls of the coverlet as her hips bucked against him, demanding that he put an end to the torture.

He couldn't deny her even that for long. As her breath grew shallow and her sounds pleading, he drew his tongue up to caress her clit. Within seconds, he felt her burst into orgasm. But he didn't stop there, he licked and sucked and did everything he could think of to draw out the convulsions slamming through her. It was magical, bringing her so much pleasure. Few things had ever made him feel so powerful, so much like a man. And when she was done coming apart, when she lay there, spent and gasping for breath, he crawled back onto the bed with her, cradling her in his arms.

"I think we will live a long and immensely satisfying life together," he whispered against her ear. "I think we will give each other everything we need."

"Yes," she agreed with a sigh, sliding her hands along his arms as they embraced her. "Felix."

"And do you know what?" he asked, mischief making one last appearance before exhaustion overtook him. "I think we should start that life by catching a diamond thief together."

CHAPTER 8

The afternoon Jo spent with Felix left her feeling as though she were floating on clouds in the sunshine. He was far more fascinating than she had given him credit for and, for a change, she was happy with the ridiculous decision her mother had made without her to bundle her off in marriage to Felix. Whatever her mother expected the deal to be, Jo was certain her life with Felix would be filled with joy, excitement, and pleasure.

That excitement was set to begin immediately. They'd spent a good portion of the rest of their afternoon discussing the diamond theft and ways they might catch the thief red-handed. Jo was startled to learn that Felix suspected a man that she and Caro—and perhaps even Rebecca's Nigel—didn't even know about—a Mr. Saif Khan, son of the Mr. Khan who managed the house.

"I'm certain he's the man we saw—" She gestured to

the wall as she and Caro moved the wardrobe early on Friday night.

"You may very well be right," Caro said, though without the same enthusiasm Jo felt. "But Saif Khan only recently returned to the house. How could he be involved in the theft?"

They managed to move the wardrobe enough to open the secret door. Jo skipped across the room, fetching lit candles, then entered the passageway with Caro.

"Felix believes there to be more than one thief," she whispered. "At least, he believes whoever stole the diamond on the day it went missing had help from an accomplice on the outside."

Caro hummed as if considering the possibility. "That seems like the most logical possibility. And we both know Miss Dobson is involved."

Jo winced at the mention of Miss Dobson. The woman had taken a turn in the last few days that could only be explained by madness or guilt. Or both. Jo had snuck back into the school through the kitchens after her day spent with Felix, fully expecting to catch the full force of Miss Dobson's wrath at her absence. The prospect was far less daunting than it would have been, considering she and Felix had talked about the possibility and he'd vowed to take her in immediately, that night, if Miss Dobson caused trouble. At heart, Jo hoped and prayed Miss Dobson would cause a scene, but when Jo crept up into the dining room in time to slide onto the bench next to Caro as their unappetizing supper of thin stew and pale bread was served, Miss Dobson was nowhere in sight.

"She will be present this evening, I know it," Caro went on as they edged their way through the secret passageway toward the room where Felix would be waiting for them. "Something is afoot this evening, and there is no doubt at all in my mind that she will be involved."

"Agreed," Jo whispered.

Once again, Miss Dobson had behaved with extreme suspicion that evening. She had rushed her few remaining pupils through supper, then sent them all up to their rooms for what she called "Evening Reflection". But the moment everyone was tucked away in their rooms, she had gone around locking doors. The past few weeks had taught Jo that when Miss Dobson locked her young ladies in, it meant she was going out.

"Here we are," Jo said when they reached the door to the appointed room—the one where Rebecca had first seen the diamond thief, or at least his backside. She slid open the peephole to be certain and was rewarded with the sight of Felix pacing the room, dressed to the nines. Her heart flipped happily in her chest, but her elation was cut short at the sight of a second man. "Someone is with him," she hissed.

Caro frowned and nudged Jo out of the way. As she looked through the peephole, her puzzled expression melted into a wicked grin. "It's Lord Herrington," she told Jo before searching out the latch to the door leading into the room.

Jo was far less at ease about entering a room from a secret passageway with a man she knew nothing about—indeed, a man who had been a suspect in the diamond theft—than Caro was, but she was so happy to have Felix instantly sweep her into his arms and plant a ravishing kiss full on her mouth that her reticence was soon forgotten.

"I have half a mind to abandon the investigation in favor of the sort of activity Khan's parties are renowned for," he said, then kissed her again.

"If we do what we've come here for quickly, there will be time for all that later," Lord Herrington said, sending a saucy wink Caro's way.

Caro responded with a coquettish blush and a look that said she wouldn't turn away that kind of attention. More than that, she flirted with Lord Herrington as though they'd known each other much longer than a handful of seconds. For the first time, Jo wondered what Caro had done to distract the man when they'd encountered him the night Rebecca was held captive in the wine cellar and she'd run on to fetch Nigel.

"I've brought gowns for you to change into," Felix said, letting go of Jo at last and assuming a businesslike air. "We can't have you flitting about a revelry like the one downstairs in mousy school uniforms."

"No," Jo agreed. "What did you bring?"

Felix crossed to two large boxes resting on the odd-shaped chaise in the center of the room and opened the lid of one. He drew out the most exquisite gown of fine, blue muslin that Jo had ever seen. The material was so fine that it felt like liquid in her hands as she took the dress from him. The whole thing was embroidered with silver leaves and flowers. A matching pair of silver slippers rested in the box.

"It's exquisite," Jo gasped, turning to Felix with an appreciative smile. "How will I ever be able to repay you for something like this."

"I can think of a few ways," Felix said with a rake's grin. "Nothing is too good for my countess."

"This is too much," Caro said in a voice laced with as much awe as Jo had felt. She'd opened the lid of the other box and now held a gown as exquisite as Jo's in a luscious shade of vermillion.

"You'll draw every eye in the place," Lord Herrington told her. "Mine especially."

"Is that so?" Caro asked, one eyebrow raised.

Lord Herrington sidled closer to her. "Do you need assistance donning your gown?"

Before Caro could answer, Felix drawled, "I've never known you to offer to help a woman put clothes on."

Lord Herrington looked abashed and laughed at himself. "You're right. But we should hurry. We all need to be in costume and mingling among Khan's guests as soon as possible if we are to unravel this mystery tonight."

"We can return to our room to change," Jo said, stepping toward the closed door of the secret passageway.

"There isn't time," Felix said. "You can change here. And we can be of assistance." When Jo looked shocked, he went on with, "It's nothing I haven't already seen."

"But...." Jo sent a glance Lord Herrington's way.

"Now is not the time to be modest," Caro said, laying her dress across the chaise so that she could reach behind her back to undo the ties of her uniform.

Jo's dropped her hesitance, handing her gown to Felix before beginning her own process of disrobing. Removing her clothes in a room with two men, only one of whom was her fiancé, seemed like the least mad thing she'd done of late.

"The best way to catch the diamond thief is to observe the behavior of those men we suspect and to stay close to them throughout the night," Felix said as the ladies disrobed.

"Who do we suspect other than Saif?" Lord Herrington asked. He appeared to be having a battle of conscience that involved serious attempts not to look at Caro as she stepped out of her uniform and petticoat and serious failures to do so.

"There's a whole list," Felix said with a sigh. "Lord Cavanaugh is a known scoundrel who associates with criminals. Monsieur Duval has made known he will stop at nothing to restore the fortunes of his family in the wake of the Revolution. Mr. Newman's factory is failing, and he's desperate to infuse it with cash."

"How can a factory possibly fail these days," Jo said dismissively as she tossed her uniform aside.

"Mismanagement," Felix answered, his eyes dropping to her mostly exposed bosom. He grinned and licked his lips as though remembering what she tasted like before continuing with, "He paid himself far too much before bothering to pay his employees or maintain his equipment."

"Every man's equipment needs maintenance," Lord Herrington added. Jo noticed he was staring freely at Caro as she exchanged her drab, woolen stockings for silk ones. "Lubrication, for example, to keep the pistons—"

His randy comment was cut short as the door to the hall suddenly flung open. The man Jo was reasonably certain was Saif Khan entered the room with a smile as she yelped and ducked behind Felix.

"I knew I would catch the two of you up to no good," Saif Khan said with a sly twinkle in his eyes. "And the party has only barely begun."

Lord Herrington swept Caro—still mostly undressed —into his arms, but Jo couldn't tell if he was attempting to shelter her from Saif Khan's prying gaze or if he simply wanted to take advantage of the situation to hold her salaciously.

"Do you mind?" Felix asked, pivoting so that he could take Jo into his arms a similar way. He pulled the strap of her chemise down to expose her shoulder and far more of her breast than Jo cared to show to a stranger. "We were just getting started."

"Excellent." Saif Khan clapped his hands together,

then began unbuttoning his jacket. "I've arrived just in time. Three on two?"

A knife of genuine fear sliced through Jo's gut. Felix wouldn't actually let the man touch her or Caro, would he?

"This is a private engagement," Felix said, putting Jo a bit more at ease. "Invitation only."

Saif Khan laughed, redoing his buttons. "I was merely jesting with you," he said. "And besides, there isn't time for a dalliance, though I truly wish there was."

"Not time?" Lord Herrington asked. He had Caro wrapped around him, one of her legs hitched over his hip, and his hand on her backside with only the thin cotton of her chemise between them.

"There's never time," Saif Khan said with a laugh that struck Jo's ears as suspicious. "Society never sleeps and the wheels of invention are in constant motion."

Jo frowned at the answer, if an answer it could be called.

"Why are you up here, then?" Felix asked.

"I was looking for a vacant room," Saif Khan answered. "Obviously, my search continues."

"I see," Felix said in a tight voice.

"I'll leave you to your orgy," Saif Khan continued, backing toward the door. "But if I were you, I'd tup these strumpets and hurry downstairs with all haste. Not only has my father provided a wide array of tasty morsels to feast on, Lord Somerset is here." He laughed. "A bloody duke!"

"Somerset?" Lord Herrington asked with a frown.

"Yes, so hurry along." Saif Khan made a final, extraordinarily rude gesture before fleeing to the hallway and shutting the door behind him.

He left Jo and Caro, and likely the gentlemen as well, thoroughly baffled in his wake.

"There's only one thing Saif could possibly need a vacant room for," Felix said, letting Jo out of his arms and helping her to continue dressing with all haste. He held the magnificent gown for her as she stepped in, as competent as the finest lady's maid.

"He either plans to discuss the diamond tonight or to sell it outright," Lord Herrington said.

"If he is in possession of it," Caro added. Lord Herrington helped her slide into her gown as Felix helped Jo. Whatever boundaries of propriety existed, they were gone now. "Only a fool would bring the diamond itself back to the location from which it was stolen."

"And besides," Jo said, shimmying so that her gown fell into place, then turning her back to Felix so that he could do it up, "when we heard the thief speaking to Miss Dobson, he said the diamond is safe where it is, in the hands of a friend."

"But you also informed me Miss Dobson's buyer wanted to see what he might purchase," Felix said. "And days have passed since that conversation. Further arrangements could have been made."

"I don't think we can rule out the possibility that the

diamond is here," Lord Herrington agreed. "Which means we must proceed with caution and sharp attention to everything around us." His gaze settled on Caro's chest —which looked close to spilling out the front of her gown once it was fastened and in place.

"Believe me, Lord Herrington, we will not let anything escape our notice," Caro agreed, her own gaze dropping to the defined bulge in Lord Herrington's breeches.

Felix chuckled, then shook his head. "We need to act now, before we change our minds about our purpose for being here and succumb to temptation."

Truer words could not have been spoken. Jo took Felix's hand as he headed toward the door. The moment they stepped into the hallway, it was as though the mantle of purpose had descended on her. She had a job to do, and she would do it well.

"We should split up," Felix said as they made their way down the stairs to the ground floor. Already, the sounds of music and laughter were filtering up through the house. "We'll be able to see more that way."

"Agreed," Lord Herrington said.

That was the last Jo heard from him as they arrived in the ballroom. Within seconds, Lord Herrington whisked Caro off into the room writhing with people of every description. Jo had witnessed one of Mr. Khan's grand parties through the secret passageway in the past few weeks, but that sort of concealment was nothing compared to being thrust into the heart of the whirlwind itself. The ballroom was pulsing with life and excitement. It held the same number and concentration of people as she'd experienced during her one and only trip to Almack's, but the feeling in the air was decidedly different. Rather than the brittle manners of the ton, Mr. Khan's party was heady with sensuality. The scent of perfume and musk filled the air. Couples stood too close, laughed too loud. More than a few of the ladies exposed far more than would ever have been proper in polite society. It was almost enough to make Jo feel overdressed, even though the neckline of the gown Felix had given her was so low that the tips of her areolas peeked out above the silver embroidery.

"And Mr. Khan hosts revels like this frequently?" Jo whispered as Felix escorted her around the perimeter of the crowded room. They received more than a few hungry glances from men and women alike as they paraded.

"All the time," Felix said, his lazy smile clearly an act to hide the spark of observation in his eyes. "He's quite famous for it. Anyone in search of casual debauchery pays quite a sum to remain on Khan's guest list."

She glanced away from a rather large woman who was receiving a great deal of glowing appreciation for her exposed expanses of flesh and stared at him. "And you are one of those men?" she asked, one eyebrow arched.

Felix laughed, but this time the sound held a good deal of sheepishness. "I do business with the East India Company. I invest with them. They've made me quite a bit of money. So I am on their guest list as a matter of course."

"I see," she said, believing him, but putting on a teasing, skeptical look all the same.

"I'll stop coming at once, of course," he said, holding her a little closer as they reached a spot that would give them a clear view of the entire room. "One has no need of the hunt when they have already captured the prey."

It was Jo's turn to laugh. "And what if I want to attend festivities such as this? You forget that I've seen what transpires at these events through the walls. What if I want to participate as well?"

He tugged her close—so close that, were they anywhere else, his embrace would have been seen as deadly scandalous—and slipped one hand into her bodice to squeeze her breast. "I'll bring you here as often as you'd like and whisk you off to whatever secluded spot you wish to fuck you silly. It's quite invigorating when you run the risk of being discovered by any number of people mid-rut."

They absolutely shouldn't have, but his words sent shivers of lust through her. There must have been something terribly wrong with her, considering how aroused she was to have him handling her with overt sexuality in a crowded ballroom. Several men and women were watching openly as he rubbed her nipple into a hard point, then withdrew his hand from her bodice, leaving her pert nub exposed to all. Perhaps she was every bit as wicked as her mother believed her to be after all.

She was within a hair's breadth of begging him to take her back up to the room where they'd changed and to bury his cock deep within her when he said, with utter seriousness, "Observe."

With a supreme effort, Jo dragged herself out of the haze of lust she'd fallen into and followed the line of his gaze. At the other side of the room, near the small orchestra playing all manner of instruments, including some Jo had never seen before, Saif Khan was in deep discussion with Mr. Newman. In a room full of people wearing expressions of carnality and enjoyment, their seriousness stuck out like a sore thumb.

"Mr. Newman," Jo whispered. Caro had suspected him as the thief from the start. Could she be right?

Jo searched the room for her friend and found her in a corner with Lord Herrington. He sat against the arm of a long sofa, Caro straddling him. She had one slippered foot up on the sofa and her entire leg was exposed as Lord Herrington stroked it intimately. Jo's jaw dropped, but just as she was tempted to believe Caro had abandoned their mission to misbehave with Lord Harrington, she noticed the gravity of Lord Herrington's expression as he whispered in her ear. His eyes were trained on Saif Khan and Mr. Newman as well. They were as aware of the situation as Jo and Felix were.

"What do we do?" Jo whispered, panic swirling through the other, nicer emotions coursing through her. The jumble was overwhelming.

"We wait and watch to see what they do," Felix murmured to her.

Jo supposed that was all they could do. She did her best to pretend to be a lust-addled ninny, plying herself against Felix as though she wanted nothing more than for him to lift her skirts and fiddle with her in full view of the rest of the guests. Felix played along, pretending not to be interested in anything else but sampling her favors...and giving the guests around them quite a show. One particularly disturbing, older gentlemen began openly rubbing his breeches when Felix tugged her sleeve down her arm and began kissing her shoulder.

"Can we move somewhere else?" Jo whispered. "That man is frightening me."

"Certainly," Felix said. He slid his arm through hers and beat a speedy retreat through the ballroom, heading for the door.

Across the room, Saif Khan broke away from Mr. Newman. Neither man resumed the carefree air of the rest of the guests. Saif Khan appeared to be headed toward the door. He reached the hall and disappeared before Jo and Felix were halfway across the ballroom. Adding to their dilemma, the man who had been watching them was following.

"What could he possibly be after?" Jo hissed as they picked up their pace and dodged through the party guests and into the hall.

"There's a fair chance he will ask to watch us or participate if he catches up to us," Felix said.

Jo squealed in disgust. "Hurry. We need to hide."

Felix nodded, whisking her into the hall, then rushing along to a door several dozen yards down and on the other side from the ballroom. He pulled it open and tugged Jo inside, shutting the door behind them.

Jo was ready to breathe a sigh of relief at their narrow escape, but the moment she turned around to survey the room, she was met with an entirely different, far bigger problem.

Miss Dobson—dressed as scantily as any of the other female party guests—stood from the chair where she'd been sitting, a look of shock and alarm on her wrinkled face. Her jaw dropped, and she demanded, "What are you doing here?"

CHAPTER 9

Few things were as disconcerting to Felix as discovering too late that he should have planned better. He was a fool to think that he and Josephine would be able to pick out the diamond thief from among Khan's party guests, and that as soon as the man was identified, he would be able to swoop in like a hero of legend, apprehend him, and expose his indiscretions to the world. Saif and Newman were behaving suspiciously, but he could do little about it standing on the opposite side of a ballroom and even less by whisking Josephine out of the room and away from a different sort of threat altogether. Lord Hazelton was a notorious libertine, and Felix had no intention of giving the man the slightest notion that he and Josephine would indulge his penchant for voyeurism.

But Lord Hazelton turned out to be the least of his worries.

"What are you doing here?"

He whipped around at the gasped question only to find Miss Dobson—mistress of the so-called school Josephine attended, who also happened to be the illegitimate daughter of the Duke of Somerset—gaping at Josephine.

"I...that is...Felix invited me...." Josephine struggled to explain herself.

Felix stepped in front of her, drawing himself up to his full height. "Miss Hodges is here as my guest. If you make an issue of that fact, I will withdraw her from your school immediately."

He expected indignation and protest. What he received was a look of sheer panic from Miss Dobson. She launched toward Josephine, waving her arms and making a desperate sound.

"You must leave at once," she squeaked at last, glancing over her shoulder to a door at the far end of the room. It was a large, public room, decorated lavishly with gilded sofas and chairs. A golden statue of the god Ganesh with a ruby in his forehead stood on the mantel, as if he were there to supervise official meetings. Miss Dobson was clearly there for a meeting of a sinister sort. "You cannot be here, not now."

Felix's nerves bristled. Josephine and her friend had sworn that Miss Dobson was involved in the diamond theft, and her actions seemed to prove it.

"We are not going anywhere," he declared. "Not

until you confess to being an accomplice in the theft of the Chandramukhi Diamond."

Miss Dobson shrieked and reeled back, clutching a hand to her chest. "How did you know?" she gasped, then immediately shook her head and changed her tune. "I didn't steal anything. I didn't know about it until after the fact. It's not my fault that I was embroiled in the fiasco. I only—" She slapped a hand over her mouth as though she'd said too much.

"You confess, then?" Josephine said, eyes wide, stepping toward Miss Dobson. "You confess to assisting in a criminal act?"

"Yes. No! I would never...." Miss Dobson gaped for a moment before her expression hardened. "What are you doing out of your room? I locked the door myself. How did you—"

Her question was cut off as the door Miss Dobson had been glancing toward opened and Newman stepped through. Almost simultaneously, a section of the wall on the opposite side of the room clicked, a door like the one Josephine and Lady Caroline had come through upstairs swung inward, and Saif stepped into the room. He started at the sight of Felix and Jo, or perhaps Miss Dobson, or even Newman.

A moment later, Saif broke into a wry grin. "Isn't this a party," he said, rubbing his hands together. "Are we playing three on two after all?"

No one had a chance to answer. As soon as the question was out of Saif's mouth, the door Felix and Josephine had entered through swung open once more to reveal the ruddy face and protruding form of Lord Hazelton.

"Good," Hazelton said, beginning to unfasten his breeches. "You haven't started yet."

"No," Josephine yelped with a level of offense that would have been charming in any other situation.

Her cry echoed through the room as though it were a clap of thunder spooking a corral of horses. Everybody moved at once. Newman dashed back through the door he'd appeared through. Saif's jovial expression vanished as he leapt into the secret passageway once more. Miss Dobson screamed and barreled straight toward Felix and Josephine. When Felix lifted Josephine out of the way, she tore right past them, past Lord Hazelton, and into the hallway.

"They're getting away," Josephine shouted.

"We'll go after them," Felix said. He grabbed her hand and darted toward the door Miss Dobson had left through.

"They've gone in three different directions," Josephine said.

"I'm not going anywhere," Lord Hazelton said as Felix and Josephine rushed past. His breeches were already undone, and Felix didn't want to think about the flash of pink he'd seen poking out from the tails of his shirt.

They ran into the hall in time to see Miss Dobson disappear around the corner, heading to the front of the house. Felix chased after her, still holding tightly to

Josephine's hand. "We have to alert Rufus," he said, keeping his eyes peeled for any sight of Saif or Newman. "He can chase as well."

"But who?" Josephine asked, panting.

It was a powerful question, one he didn't have the time to pause and answer.

They rounded the corner into the front hall just as the front door slammed shut. Someone—Miss Dobson, if he was right—had fled the building. Fortunately for them, Rufus and Lady Caroline sped out into the hall from the ballroom only a moment later.

"We interrupted something," Felix said, as they all met in the center of the hall. "Miss Dobson fled. Newman appeared to be there to meet her."

"Where is he?" Lady Caroline asked.

"I don't know," Felix told her. "He exited the room through another door. Saif was there as well. He escaped into the secret passageway."

"Who has the diamond?" Rufus asked.

"None of them had it," Josephine said. "But I am certain they were moments from revealing its where-abouts or arranging a sale."

"We have to go after them," Lady Caroline said.

Felix nodded in agreement. "We'll pursue Saif," he said.

"And we'll look for Newman," Rufus followed. He took Lady Caroline's hand and dashed toward the large refreshment room opposite the ballroom. Felix trusted his friend knew enough of the layout of the house to guess where Newman had gone.

"But what about Miss Dobson?" Josephine cried as Felix pulled her down the hall toward the room they'd just left.

"She's the least of our worries," Felix said.

He could see from her expression she wasn't convinced, but there was no time to argue.

They rounded the corner and dashed back to the private room, passing Lord Hazelton as they did.

"Are we back on?" the oafish lord asked, looking delighted.

Felix ignored him, racing into the room and over to the doorway to the secret passageway. Only, the wall seemed to be completely intact without a single sign of a door of any sort.

"They're difficult to find unless you know what you're searching for," Josephine said, leaping in front of him. She placed her hands on the room's ornate wall-paper once they were right in front of it and appeared to be scanning the design. A moment later she let out an, "Ah ha!" and pressed what seemed like a random spot on the paper.

To Felix's immense relief, the door clicked and swung inward. He didn't hesitate. He leapt through into darkness, taking Josephine's hand and drawing her in with him.

"One moment," she cautioned him, leaping back out into the room. She returned a half second later with a three-pronged candelabra. "The passages are pitch dark."

Felix nodded, the situation too urgent for him to say more. He closed the door behind Josephine once she was inside with him. Only then did he realize he wasn't sure where to go.

"The mews," Josephine said, edging in front of him in a way that brought the candelabra far too close to his face for comfort. "If I were running away from being discovered, I would head straight for the mews and out of the house."

"There's a way out of the house from here?" Felix asked, following her closely.

"There's more than one. Although the second exit is currently blocked by debris in the alley beside the house."

He accepted her explanation without question. No doubt Josephine and Lady Caroline had explored every inch of the passageway. He would tease her about how naughty it was to sneak through someone else's house another time. For now, he needed her expertise.

Evidently, Saif could have used her expertise as well. He must have been navigating the passageway in the dark, for as Felix and Josephine turned a corner and reached the passage that Josephine said led to the mews, they saw a sudden flash of night sky and felt a breath of cool air as the mews door opened.

"Saif," Felix called out, resting a hand on Josephine's back and urging her to move faster.

No answer came, and the door swung shut, but by

then they were so close that Felix had no doubt they were moments from catching Saif. And once they did, Felix had a thousand questions for his so-called friend.

But when they reached the door, it stuck. Josephine stepped back to allow Felix to go first, but the door remained stuck. Felix threw his shoulder into it, and it budged a bit. He slammed into it again, and it opened a bit more. A few more crashing blows were enough to reveal that a heavy barrel had been rolled in front of the door. Once Felix was able to get that out of the way, allowing him and Josephine to run into the mews, Saif was nowhere to be seen.

"Dammit," Felix hissed under his breath, balling his hands into fists.

"Over there." Josephine pointed toward one of the rows of stalls with her free hand.

Felix pivoted in time to see a shadowy figure on a dark horse leap out of a stall and charge down the alley to the mews' exit.

"Was that him?" Josephine asked.

"Who else would it be?" Felix answered, taking her hand and running toward the exit. There was little chance they would catch Saif, but they had to—

"Friends! Where are you going?"

Felix skidded to a stop and jerked around, searching for the source of the voice that echoed through the mews. Josephine's gasp as she glanced back toward the house drew him in the right direction. A first-floor window was open and Wakas Khan leaned out, his sherwani fully unbuttoned to expose a chest that was surprisingly muscular for a man of his age.

"Where are you going?" he called again, laughter in his voice. The Wyncoll twins, both clearly naked, their blonde hair loose over their shoulders, appeared on either side of him, reaching inside his unbuttoned sherwani to stroke his chest. "There are pleasures of all kinds to be enjoyed here tonight."

Felix frowned, suspicion firing within him. "We're looking for your son," he said.

"Bah." Khan made a dismissive gesture. "My son is a disgrace. He piles up debt through gambling and bad investment and expects me to save him. Let him sort things for himself this time. I have far better things to—" His words changed to a strangled gasp, then a laugh, as one of the twins reached for something Felix was glad he couldn't see below the man's waist.

There was no point in questioning Khan further. In fact, he was wasting their time. "Come on," Felix said, pulling Josephine into motion once more.

"Could he be helping Saif Khan?" Josephine asked the very question Felix was thinking as they rounded the corner and dashed from the mews into Manchester Square.

"He could," Felix answered.

Manchester Square was as sleepy as it ever was at that time of night. The square was lined with carriages that had brought people to Khan's entertainment. The drivers clustered together, passing the time until their employers wandered out of the reveries. There were as many carriages waiting on the north end of the square, outside of Hertford House, as there were in front of the East India Company's house, a fact which alarmed Felix. Saif could easily have escaped one raucous party by inviting himself into a second party. The Marquess of Hertford was generous in his guest list.

"What do we do?" Josephine asked.

Felix wished he had an authoritative answer to her question. The fact of the matter was, he was at a loss.

He was only saved somewhat when Rufus and Lady Caroline came dashing toward them from the other side of the East India Company's house.

"Newman is nowhere to be found," Rufus said, out of breath, face red from exertion.

"We thought we'd caught up with him only a moment after we parted ways," Lady Caroline added, equally breathless. "But he seemed to know what we were after as soon as he spotted us, and he ran."

"Saif Khan appears to have gotten away as well," Josephine said, disappointment lacing her voice.

Felix felt as though he had failed her. Or perhaps he'd been a fool to think he could catch a diamond thief in the first place. "If either Saif or Newman is the thief, we've tipped our hand. They'll know we suspect them now."

"If I were either one of them, I would return home or leave the country with all due haste," Rufus agreed.

"We should have told Rebecca what we were going to

do," Josephine said. "That way, she could have asked Nigel how we should go about doing it."

"I'm beginning to think it would have been wise to approach the Bow Street Runners with what we know to begin with," Rufus agreed.

Felix ran a hand through his hair in frustration. "They suspect us, you know," he said.

"But you're not guilty," Josephine insisted. "And I can prove it." Felix eyed her sideways, warmed by her faith in him but uncertain she would be considered a strong enough witness to vouch for his innocence, until she went on with, "You don't have the birthmark, remember?"

"The birthmark," Lady Caroline exclaimed. "I'd almost forgotten."

"What birthmark?" Rufus asked.

"The thief bears a birthmark in the shape of a half-moon on his backside," Lady Caroline said, sending a sly grin Rufus's way. "Rebecca witnessed it herself. Any man without said birthmark can be automatically ruled out as a suspect."

"Is that so?" Rufus asked, his eyebrow twitching as he sent her a saucy smile. "My lady, would you care to witness my innocence in this theft? I feel it only right to reassure you that you have not thrown your lot in with a notorious jewel thief."

Lady Caroline bit her lip, her eyes dancing with eagerness. Felix was fairly certain she would have taken Rufus up on his offer instantly if the door to the school hadn't flown open at precisely that moment. All four of them turned in time to see Miss Dobson, poorly concealed with a cloak around her shoulders, its hood up, dashing down the stairs with a clumsy bag under one arm. She stumbled at the bottom of the stairs, but recovered fast enough to take off in the direction of Oxford Street.

"Stop," Josephine shouted. "Where do you think you're going?"

Felix was forced to follow, Rufus with him, as Josephine and Lady Caroline chased after Miss Dobson. Miss Dobson yelped when she realized she was being chased and picked up her pace. Felix and Rufus outpaced the ladies within a few yards, and Felix was certain they would catch Miss Dobson easily, but she surprised them by cutting between two parked carriages and into the street.

"Stop her," Josephine shouted again.

Her cry was in vain. A third carriage was waiting on the other side of the two parked ones. Its door was open, and with a swift and surprisingly agile movement, Miss Dobson threw her bag inside, then leapt toward the door as the carriage lurched into motion. A pair of masculine arms reached out to drag her all the way inside as the carriage picked up speed. Felix and Rufus dashed between the two parked carriages and into the street, but it was too late. The carriage door snapped shut, and the driver whipped the horses into top speed. The carriage disappeared around Hinde Street and was gone.

"What the devil just happened?" Rufus asked as he and Felix stood in the street, panting and in shock.

A passing carriage driver whistled for the two of them to make way, and they jogged back to the sidewalk, where Josephine and Lady Caroline were standing, looking utterly baffled.

"She got away," Lady Caroline said, clearly frustrated.

"She left." Josephine shook her head. "She simply left."

"How involved in the diamond plot was she?" Rufus asked.

"She was the one who arranged for the thief to sell the diamond," Lady Caroline said, wincing in frustration. "We heard her the other day. She said a friend of her father's, a collector, was interested in purchasing it."

"I'm certain that's what the meeting we happened upon was about," Josephine said. "And now it's too late. All three of them have escaped."

"The thief, the buyer, and Miss Dobson," Felix said, raking a hand through his hair, irritated enough to pull it out.

"So who was who?" Rufus asked. "Miss Dobson, we know. But is Newman the thief or is it Saif?"

"Neither have the money to buy something of that price," Felix thought aloud. "So the buyer must be someone else, someone who hadn't arrived before it fell apart."

"That still doesn't answer the question of who stole

the diamond and who may have simply been in the wrong place at the wrong time," Rufus said.

"And it certainly doesn't explain where the diamond is at present," Lady Caroline answered.

The four of them stood there in disappointed silence for a moment, until Josephine asked, "What do we do next?"

"I'm afraid we'll have to do what we should have done from the start," Felix said. "We'll have to contact Mr. Kent and the Bow Street Runners to apprise them of the situation."

"And what about the school?" Josephine asked on.

Felix blinked. "The school?"

Josephine shrugged. "Miss Dobson is gone. The school has been abandoned. But there are at least twenty young ladies still in its care, without any place to go."

"I'll take care of them," Lady Caroline said, stepping closer to Josephine. "Most of us are old enough to fend for ourselves, though some organization is in order, I'm certain. And if our families fail to be notified of the situation, all the better. You go with Lord Lichfield." Mischief was bright in the young noblewoman's face.

Josephine turned to Felix. "Would you mind?" she asked in a small voice.

"Mind?" he laughed. "That would be the one thing that could turn this misery of an evening into something good."

Josephine blushed, then handed the candelabra to

Lady Caroline. "I won't be needing this," she said before skipping to Felix's side and taking his arm.

"My lady," Felix told her, resting his hand over hers with a tired smile. "From now on, I will see to it that you do not need anything. It will all be yours."

CHAPTER 10

*J*o should have been disappointed at the way the events of the evening had unfolded, but that was impossible to do when Felix whisked her into the carriage he had waiting down the road and carried her off to his home. His proper home, not the secret address designed for clandestine assignations.

"Let the gossip-mongers talk," he told her, lifting her across his lap and wrapping his arms around her as the carriage jostled through the night. "They've said more than enough about me already. And if word gets out that I brought my countess home to bed a few days before the wedding, well, all I can say to that is that money and a title go a long way towards hushing rumors."

Jo giggled, but that quickly turned into a sigh. "It's a shame that it is so," she said. "Too many of the young ladies at Miss Dobson's school—or do you suppose it's

Caro's school now—have been shunted off into obscurity because they have either a title or money but not both?"

"If your friend, Lady Caroline, continues on with the school, I pledge to support it and its pupils to the best of my ability and to ensure the young ladies there are given the introduction to society they deserve," he said.

Jo's heart filled with sunshine that felt as though it would lift her through the roof of the carriage and into the starry sky above. "Oh, Felix, you are wonderful."

She leaned into him, kissing him with a boldness that surprised her before he could say anything self-effacing. It felt wonderful to be so free with him and to give full vent to the passion she felt without having him judge her or assume she was of low moral character. As she teased her tongue tentatively into his mouth, she began to understand that there was a world of difference between sharing her favors with any man who wanted them and being sensual and alive with a man she loved.

As soon as the thought struck her, she gasped and jerked back.

"What?" Felix asked, his eyes heavy-lidded and his voice distracted. "What is it?"

"I've just realized," Jo said, blinking in amazement. "I love you."

Felix's eyes went wide as well. "You love me?" he asked, seemingly baffled.

"Yes, I believe I do." It was so unexpected and so delightfully convenient that she burst into a laugh.

"What a wonderful thing to discover on a night such as this."

"I'll say," Felix said, his smile turning downright wolfish. He pulled her back into his arms and twisted in such a way that left her wedged against the side of the seat with one leg lifted over his hip. "One can do any number of horrifically wicked things to a woman when she loves you."

Jo's laughter turned into giddy giggles and gasps as Felix set out to prove his point. He kissed her hard, leaving her breathless and panting for more. All the while, his free hand roamed her body, tugging her skirts up well above her waist and circling her backside. That only lasted a moment before he reached up to tug the front of her gown down, exposing her breasts to his hungry mouth. How he managed to contort into just the right position to kiss and suckle her heavy, sensitive breasts was a mystery to her, but within seconds, she was hot and aching and could think of nothing more but freeing his erection so that he could join with her.

She had just worked up the courage and coordination to unfasten his breeches when the carriage lurched to a stop.

"We've arrived, my lord," the driver's muffled voice came from above.

"Excellent," Felix said, righting himself and tugging at his jacket, as if that could make him look presentable. He gazed down at Jo, her skirt bunched high enough to reveal more than a teasing glimpse of her sex and her breasts straining over the neck of her gown, their nipples hard and pink. Lust filled his gaze. "I want you naked and in my bed immediately."

Jo could only moan in response. Felix had to help her to sit and attempt to make herself presentable. Her breasts were still out when the driver opened the door. The poor one man took one look, eyes wide, then turned away, red growing on his cheeks. Felix met Jo's eyes with a guilty grin and helped her to tuck everything away before stepping down from the carriage and lifting her after him.

The dour butler was waiting at the door to let them in. Jo spent all of three seconds trying to remember his name before giving up and hurrying through the front hall toward the stairs with Felix.

They almost made it before a call of, "What is the meaning of this?" sounded from the doorway to a sitting room on the right.

Jo felt as though she had been struck by lightning as every nerve and muscle in her body tensed. She turned to find Lady Lichfield, Felix's mother, frowning at them. Worse still, her own mother walked up behind Lady Lichfield, her mouth dropped in shock.

"Josephine? Why aren't you at school? And what in heaven's name are you wearing?"

Jo peeked down at her gown. Outside of the exotic setting of the East India Company's house, it looked wickedly scandalous. The fabric was almost diaphanous, and try though she and Felix had, one of her nipples still popped above the neckline. Worse still, her hair was in disarray, and her lips felt swollen and red from kissing.

Her mother seemed to take in the same details. She grimaced, shaking her head, "Oh, Josephine. I should have known you were a whore."

Jo's heart began to sink, but before she could do more than let her shoulders droop, Felix took a firm, commanding step toward the mothers.

"I will not hear another word from either of you about my beloved," he said, his voice laced with fury. "You connived to marry me off without consulting me in the matter, but the fates appear to have been conspiring with you. Josephine is everything I could desire in a woman. She is clever and witty—"

"Josephine?" Jo's mother interrupted, incredulous.

Felix took a step toward her, finger pointed, and she yelped and backpedaled, grabbing Lady Lichfield's arm as she went. The two, older women huddled together.

"Not another word from either of you," Felix warned them, his voice raised. "That you chose well for me is entirely coincidental. I thank you for that, but that is all. Mother—" he turned to Lady Lichfield. "The moment Josephine and I are married—and I intend for that to be tomorrow—you will retire to the dower house at Lichfield Hall."

"But I have friends," Lady Lichfield protested, "I have social responsibilities."

"You will no longer be the countess," Felix reminded

her. "If you wish to stay in London, it will not be under this roof, do I make myself clear?"

"But...you cannot...after all I've done for you?"

"All you have done for me is look down your nose at me in distaste, condemn me for things you don't understand, and, I suspect, furthered the ruination of my reputation with your gossip," he said. "If you had ever shown me one ounce of maternal affection, we would not be in this situation."

Lady Lichfield shrank from the accusation, looking both guilty and sullen, but more than anything, defeated.

"And as for you," Felix went on, turning to Jo's mother once more. "As of tomorrow, your daughter will be a countess, which is far more than you will ever be able to say for yourself. I suggest you begin treating her with the respect she will command immediately. That means leaving this house without further comment on her appearance or character." Felix turned to Jo. "My wife-to-be is an angel in both beauty and kindness of heart. I have never met a woman as compassionate as her or as lovely. I'll have her portrait painted and placed in every room of each of my homes. I never want to be without her again."

"Oh, Felix," Jo said, blinking rapidly to fight back the tears that welled up from her heart. "You are my hero."

And right there, with both mothers looking on, he swept her into his arms and kissed her soundly. Jo molded against him, ignoring all else but the way her insides melted for him.

All too soon, he broke their kiss to say to the mothers, "Now, if you will excuse me, I am taking my wife to bed."

He clasped Jo's hand and started up the stairs even as Lady Lichfield started to say, "She's not your wife yet." She only made it through two words before giving up her efforts.

Jo didn't bother to glance over her shoulder to see what Lady Lichfield did next or if her mother left. In no time, they reached the top of the stairs and Felix picked up his pace as they raced to his bedroom.

Once they reached it and shut themselves inside, Felix backed Jo against the wall, pinning her body with his and slanting his mouth over hers with punishing force. Jo groaned at his show of dominance, lifting a leg over his hip and gripping his sides. He rewarded her efforts by jerking against her in imitation of what they would soon be doing. The hard length of his staff rubbed against her hip, making her burn in anticipation.

"I need you," she panted as he seared a trail of kisses along her neck. "I want you inside me."

"I want to make you scream when you come," he growled against her ear.

It was such an exciting comment that she wriggled against him, paradoxically pushing him away so that she could shed her clothes. He seemed to sense what she was after and stepped back, frantically working the buttons of his jacket and waistcoat as she did her best to pull at the ties to loosen her gown.

As always, infuriatingly, the complicated and all too

lengthy process of disrobing cooled the intensity of their ardor. But stepping back had its benefits.

"I was a fool to rush into our plan tonight," Felix said with a spark of naughtiness in his eyes as he pulled off his boot. He was already shirtless, the sight of him stoking the flames within Jo once more.

"We all should have planned better," she panted, stepping out of her gown and petticoats and going to work on her stays. "You were right. We should have spoken to Rebecca and Mr. Kent first."

"My over-eagerness to catch the thief led to poor decisions," he went on. As soon as he tossed his second boot aside and stood from where he'd been sitting against the bed to loosen his breeches, he added, "I deserve to be punished."

Jo had just dropped her stays to the floor and reached for the hem of her chemise, but a shiver of wicked anticipation swirled through her, making her hands shake. She met Felix's saucy stare with a fiery look of her own. "Bad boys deserve a spanking," she said.

"They do," he agreed, pushing his breeches down over his hips and legs and kicking them aside. When he straightened, his massive staff stood solidly at attention, the tip already glistening. Jo caught her breath, then moaned when he said, "I think you should spank me hard."

He turned toward the bed and braced himself against it, like he had the other day. Faint traces of the licks she'd landed on his near perfect backside still stood out against his pale flesh. Liquid heat filled Jo's sex with such intensity that she worried it would slip down her thighs. She peeled her chemise off over her head, then strode slowly up to his side.

"Have you been bad?" she asked, knowing what he would say but understanding that the more she teased and taunted him, the more intense their pleasure would be.

"So bad," he growled. "So very—"

She smacked his backside before he could finish. The blow wasn't much, though it did make her hand sting a little. She would never have the strength to cause true pain, but she wasn't sure that was what mattered.

"Bad, Felix, bad," she scolded him, spanking him hard again. "Naughty, Felix, failing to plan properly."

She rained blows across his backside, and soon enough, bright red spots shone on his flesh. He jerked and flexed with each smack, making sounds of pleasure that drove Jo to distraction. It was so overwhelming that she had to stop.

She flopped onto the bed instead, spreading her legs. "You may pleasure me now, naughty boy," she said with as superior a tone as she could manage.

Her intention was to be silly, but Felix's reaction was powerful. "Yes, mistress," he said, dropping to his knees on the floor.

As he had the other day, he yanked her to the edge of the bed and buried his face between her legs. At the same time, his hands snaked up her sides to tease her breasts. It was an awkward position, but it accomplished precisely what it was intended to. Jo's body flashed alive with pleasure as he licked and squeezed and stroked her. The pleasure was so intense, in fact, that she barely had time to sink into it before he curled his tongue around her clitoris, sending her flying off into a powerful orgasm that made her very bones shudder.

She was still soaring high in the clouds of pleasure when he stood suddenly, gripping and lifting her hips to plunge into her. His angle was exquisite, and standing meant he could thrust fast and hard. The tables turned, and he was the one mastering her. She was putty in his hands as he tupped her hard. Both of them cried and grunted and made sounds that would have a Seven Dials whore blushing, and it was perfection.

A second wave of orgasm snuck up on her, and throbbing pleasure crashed over her again. He bent forward, bracing his hands on either side of her, their bodies almost close enough to touch, and then he tensed hard, letting out a cry of completion. She wrapped her legs around him, holding him inside of her and praying his spilled seed would take hold in her womb.

A moment later, he sagged over her, and the two of them rolled to the side, tangled together on top of the bed as their passion ebbed.

"We did that all wrong," Felix panted.

Jo twisted to stare at him, eyes wide. "I would say that we did it very much right."

He laughed, moving slowly to toss the decorative

pillows off the bed and to pull down the coverings. Jo moved with him under the covers, snuggling against him as they settled.

"If you really were my mistress in that way, I would follow your orders only, not fucking you until you demanded I do so," he went on.

Jo laughed. "And I suppose if you were my master, I would have submitted to far more than a thorough drubbing."

He chuckled along with her. "We have much to learn if we want to continue with that game."

"Fortunately, we have time to learn it," she said, kissing his shoulder. "I, for one, look forward to learning the proper way to order you about."

"I'll teach you everything I know," he said, the smile he wore far too cheery for what they were discussing. "I'll show you how to restrain me to the bed and to arouse me while denying me release."

"Will you?" She couldn't help but giggle at the idea, strangely aroused by the power such play might give her.

"Yes," he said, rolling her to her back and bending to kiss her shoulder. "But I'll do the same to you. I know quite a few ways to play that game."

"I'm sure you do," she said, feigning a superior attitude. "You do realize that all of your previous experience was merely training for the way you will be with me."

For a moment, he held his breath, his eyes going wide. Then a look of pure joy burned in his expression. "I love you," he said, bending down to kiss her. He lingered there for a moment before rising and saying, "I love you more than I thought I was capable of. I thought I was thoroughly debauched and destroyed, but you understand me."

"I am beginning to understand you," Jo corrected him, her heart aching as much as her sex. "I'm certain we both have quite a ways to go still before we can say we truly understand one another."

"But you accept me as I am," he insisted, kissing her and stroking his hand down her side, leaving a trail of excitement in his wake. "Dark past and all."

"It's not the past that matters," she said, resting a hand on the side of his face. "The past formed us, but the present is where we live."

"And I want to live with you always," he insisted, full of ardor. "No matter what that looks like."

"Then you're in luck," Jo smiled, wriggling under his touch, ready to make love to him all over again. "I'm not going anywhere."

EPILOGUE

"*L*adies, we have a challenge in front of us and we must rise to it," Caro said the next morning as she addressed the remaining pupils of Miss Dobson's Finishing School.

Just over a dozen young women sat at the tables in the dining room as the kitchen staff served ham and cheeses, sausage, eggs, sweet bread with jam, and every other treat they had all been denied for so long. Miss Warren and Miss Cade sat at the far end of the table, looking wary and small, but Miss Conyer had disappeared overnight when Miss Dobson's defection had made its way through the school. Two others had fled as well, but the majority had nowhere else to go.

Which was why Caro stood at the head table, addressing those who remained.

"We have a choice before us," she said. "Stay and

attempt to gain a true education under a new regime or abandon the school entirely to return to our families."

"My family is in Italy," Lady Eliza said defiantly.

"Mine are in India," Felicity said.

A flurry of comments and shouts about where the young ladies' families were and how they had no interest in joining them there filled the room. Caro had to raise her arms to quell the sudden riot of sound.

"That is what I thought," she said with a smile. "Do we all agree to stay on and support each other?"

The young ladies exchanged looks, murmuring among each other.

"Can we get away with it?" Felicity asked. "Without a patroness?"

"I shall be the patroness," Caro said. "At least until I can find someone to sponsor the school."

In fact, she had had a missive from Jo just that morning, bright and early, saying that not only were Jo and Lord Lichfield to be married that day, Lord Lichfield had offered to sponsor the school in any way that was needed. Caro's mind had immediately gone to work conjuring up new courses of study and ways to impart practical skills to the girls that would ensure their futures. And if some of those skills were of a coquettish nature, all the better. There were more ways to win a husband than by playing the piano and singing well.

"I would love to stay here without Miss Dobson," Ophelia sighed, looking relaxed for the first time in Caro's memory. "She was horrid."

The rest of the pupils agreed...with the exception of Miss Warren and Miss Cade, who simply kept their mouths shut.

"I know as well as anyone how this school could be a haven for those of us who may be in less than desirable situations at home," Caro went on. "Which is why I pledge to do my best to keep the doors open and your parents satisfied that this is where you belong."

"Hear, hear," Eliza shouted, prompting resounding echoes from the other young ladies.

"I ask but one thing from you in return," Caro said.

The room hushed, and every face turned to her in expectation.

Caro grinned, a delicious feeling of potency spreading through her. "A theft occurred at the residence next door, the house owned by the East India Company, some weeks ago. A precious jewel, the Chandramukhi Diamond, was stolen from its rightful owners. It was intended to be a gift to the king."

"I know all about the Chandramukhi Diamond," Felicity said, sitting straighter. "My father says it's cursed."

Caro's brow shot up. She hadn't heard that. Although it would explain things.

"Rebecca was assisting her Mr. Kent, a Bow Street Runner, in his investigation of the theft," she went on. "And Jo and I were attempting to continue that investigation. We have strong reason to believe that Miss Dobson was involved in the theft."

A ripple of shock spread through the room that turned into a flurry of whispers.

"If you wish to stay here," Caro went on, "I ask that you lend your assistance in the further search for the diamond and its thief."

"Yes," Eliza called out without hesitation.

"Absolutely, yes," Felicity echoed her. The two exchanged devilish looks.

"But how can we help search for a diamond and a thief?" Ophelia asked, looking as worried as always.

"I'm certain ways and means will come to us," Caro said. "All I ask is that you be willing to pursue any leads we discover."

"Yes. We will." The cry rose up around the room. It was as though the former pupils of Miss Dobson had something to look forward to at last.

"Good," Caro said. "For now, enjoy your repast. There will be more to come in the coming days."

She stepped down from her spot and took a seat at one of the tables, tucking in to better food than she'd had in ages. And while she believed in the speech she'd made to her compatriots, there was only one person that stuck in her heart and her mind when she thought of the diamond, the investigation, and everything else—Lord Rufus Herrington. For she had a secondary mission, now that the school and the diamond were on their way to being taken care of. She fully intended to find a way to restore Lord Herrington's fortunes and to make him her own.

I hope you've enjoyed Jo and Felix's story! Are you ready for the final chapter in the theft of the Chandramuki Diamond? Can Caro put all the clues together to figure out who really stole the diamond and what they've done with it? Will Rufus be able to help her with the diamond and with her school and her future? And will Caro be able to restore the fortunes of Rufus's family to win him once and for all? Find out soon in *When the Wallflowers were Wicked* Book 6, *The Clever Strumpet*!

If you enjoyed this book and would like to hear more from me, please sign up for my newsletter! When you sign up, you'll get a free, full-length novella, *A Passionate Deception*. Victorian identity theft has never been so exciting in this story of hope, tricks, and starting over. Part of my *West Meets East* series, *A Passionate Deception* can be read as a stand-alone. Pick up your free copy today by signing up to receive my newsletter (which I only send out when I have a new release)!

Sign up here: http://eepurl.com/cbaVMH

Click here for a complete list of other works by Merry Farmer.

ABOUT THE AUTHOR

I hope you have enjoyed *The Cheeky Minx*. If you'd like to be the first to learn about when new books in the series come out and more, please sign up for my newsletter here: http://eepurl.com/cbaVMH And remember, Read it, Review it, Share it! For a complete list of works by Merry Farmer with links, please visit http://wp.me/P5ttjb-14F.

Merry Farmer is an award-winning novelist who lives in suburban Philadelphia with her cats, Torpedo, her grumpy old man, and Justine, her hyperactive new baby. She has been writing since she was ten years old and realized one day that she didn't have to wait for the teacher to assign a creative writing project to write something. It was the best day of her life. She then went on to earn not one but two degrees in History so that she would always have something to write about. Her books have reached the Top 100 at Amazon, iBooks, and Barnes & Noble, and have been named finalists in the prestigious RONE and Rom Com Reader's Crown awards.

ACKNOWLEDGMENTS

I owe a huge debt of gratitude to my awesome beta-readers, Caroline Lee and Jolene Stewart, for their suggestions and advice. And double thanks to Julie Tague, for being a truly excellent editor and assistant! Thanks also to the members of the Historical Harlots Facebook Group, who provide me with all sorts of inspiration!

Click here for a complete list of other works by Merry Farmer.

Made in the USA
Las Vegas, NV
01 November 2021